SQUIDDING AROUND

CLASS CLOWN FISH!

KEVIN SHERRY

WITH COLOR BY WES DZIOBA

graphix

AN IMPRINT OF

SCHOLASTIC

To Erin Nutsugah,
a true catch and my reel love

All rights reserved. Published by Graphix, an imprint of Scholastic Inc.,
Publishers since 1920. SCHOLASTIC, GRAPHIX, and associated logos are
trademarks and/or registered trademarks of Scholastic Inc.

Library of Congress Cataloging-in-Publication Data Available

ISBN 978-1-338-63671-0 (hardcover)
ISBN 978-1-338-63670-3 (paperback)

10 9 8 7 6 5 4 3 2 1   21 22 23 24 25

Printed in China   62

First edition, May 2021
Edited by Jenne Abramowitz
Book design by Steve Ponzo
Creative Director: Phil Falco
Publisher: David Saylor

CHAPTER 1

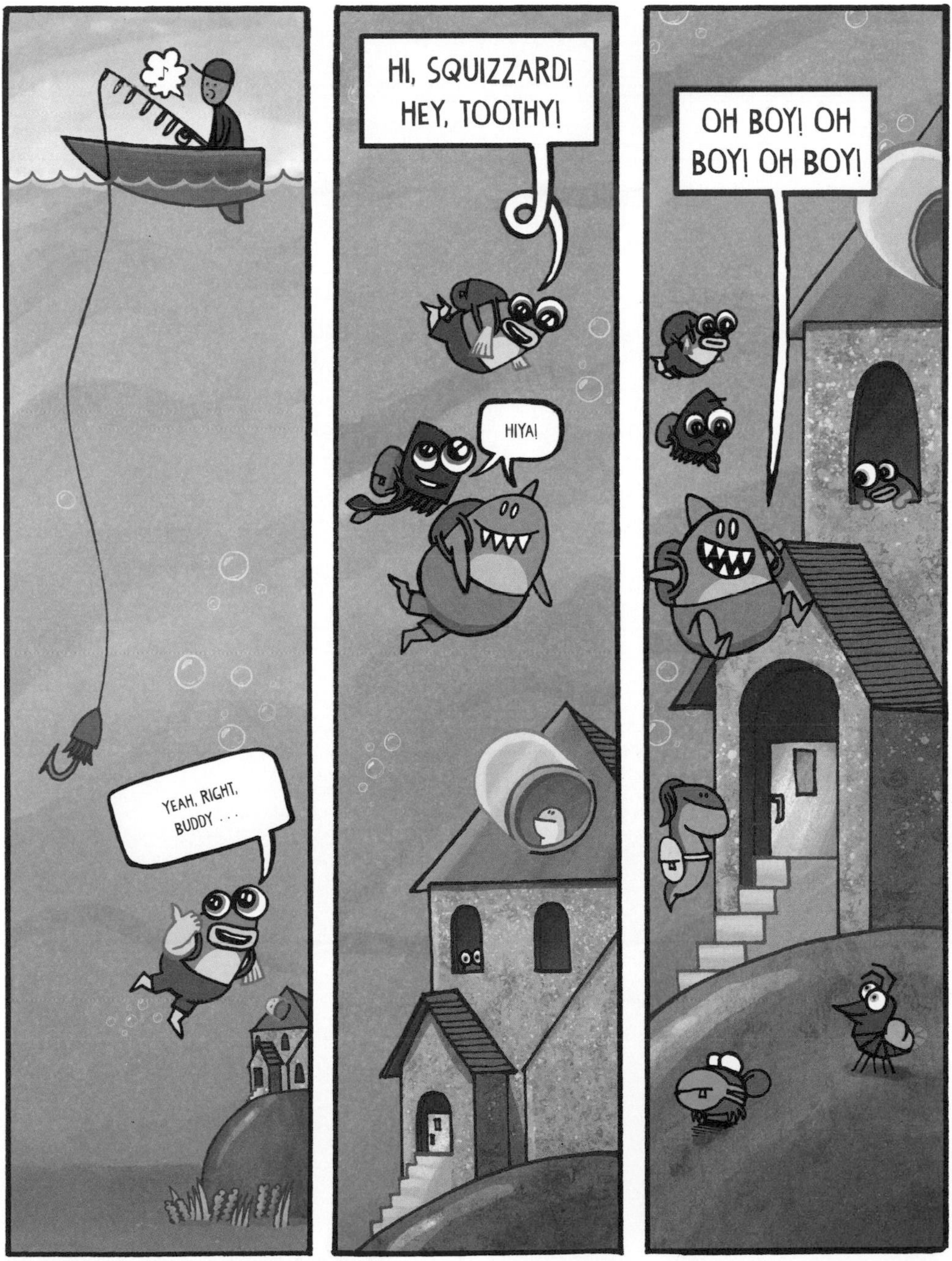
YEAH, RIGHT, BUDDY . . .
HI, SQUIZZARD! HEY, TOOTHY!
HIYA!
OH BOY! OH BOY! OH BOY!

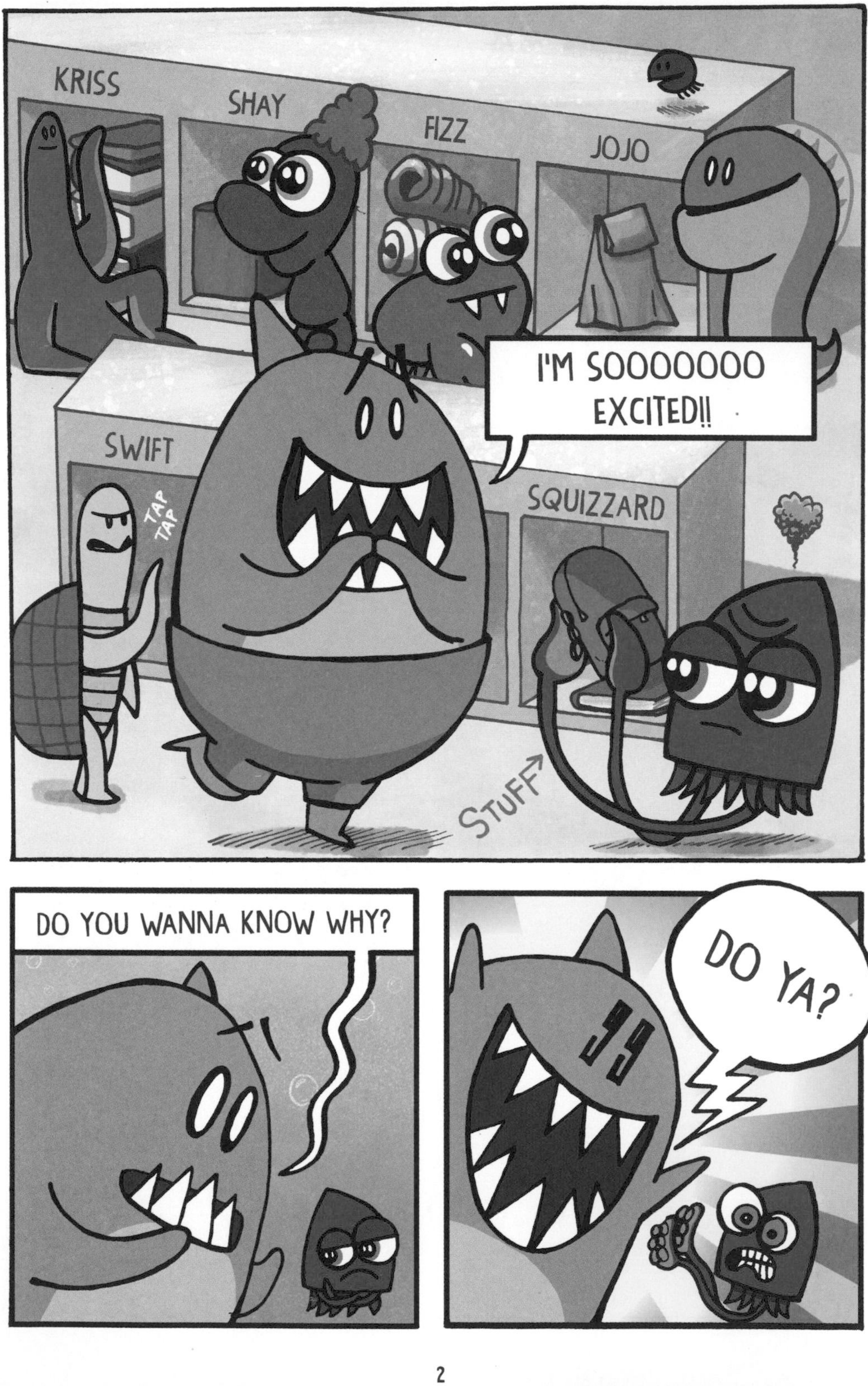
KRISS
SHAY
FIZZ
JOJO
I'M SOOOOOOO EXCITED!!
SWIFT
TAP TAP
SQUIZZARD
STUFF
DO YOU WANNA KNOW WHY?
DO YA?

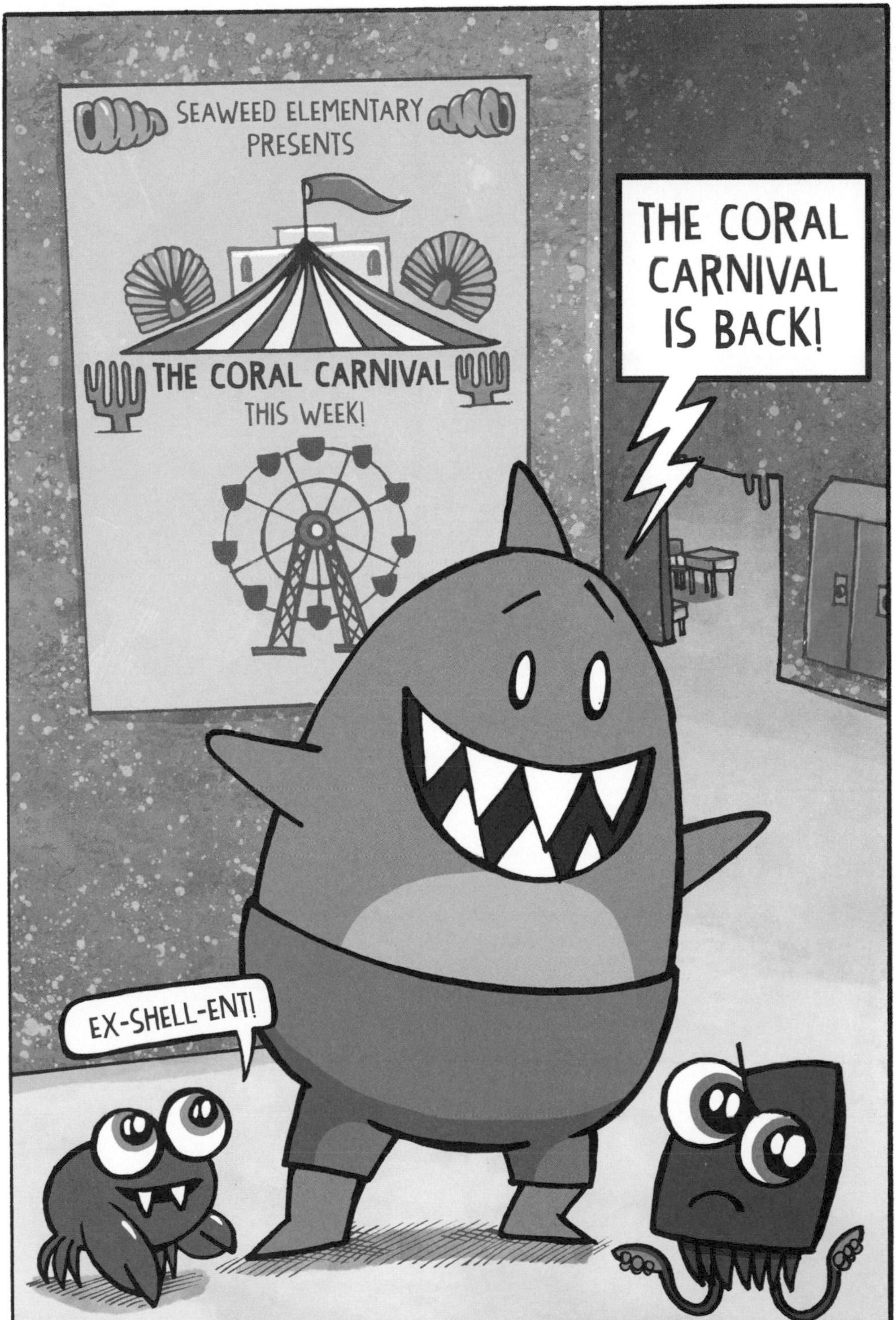
SEAWEED ELEMENTARY
PRESENTS
THE CORAL CARNIVAL
THIS WEEK!
THE CORAL CARNIVAL IS BACK!
EX-SHELL-ENT!

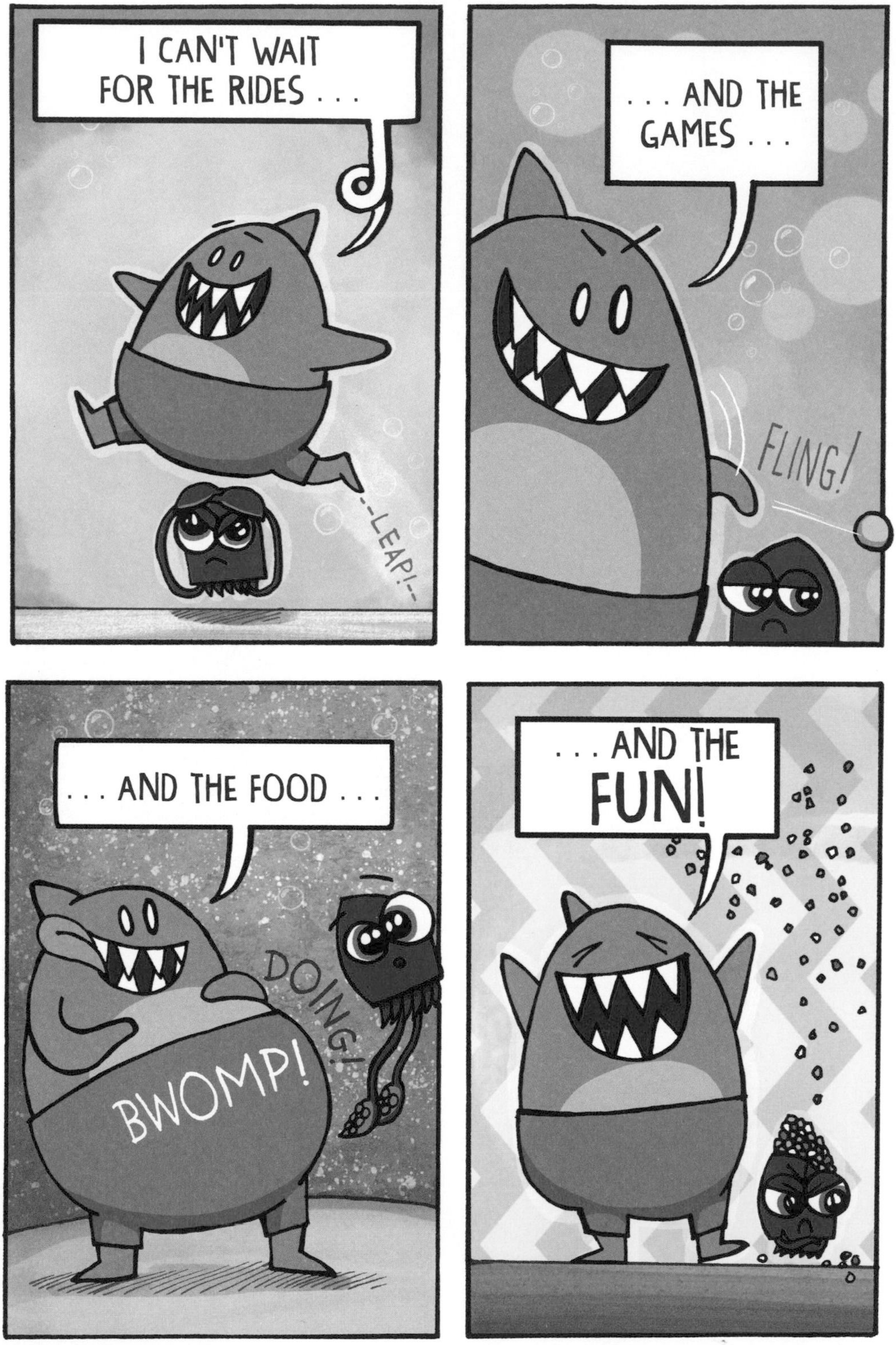
I CAN'T WAIT FOR THE RIDES . . .
LEAP!
. . . AND THE GAMES . . .
FLING!
. . . AND THE FOOD . . .
DOING!
BWOMP!
. . . AND THE FUN!

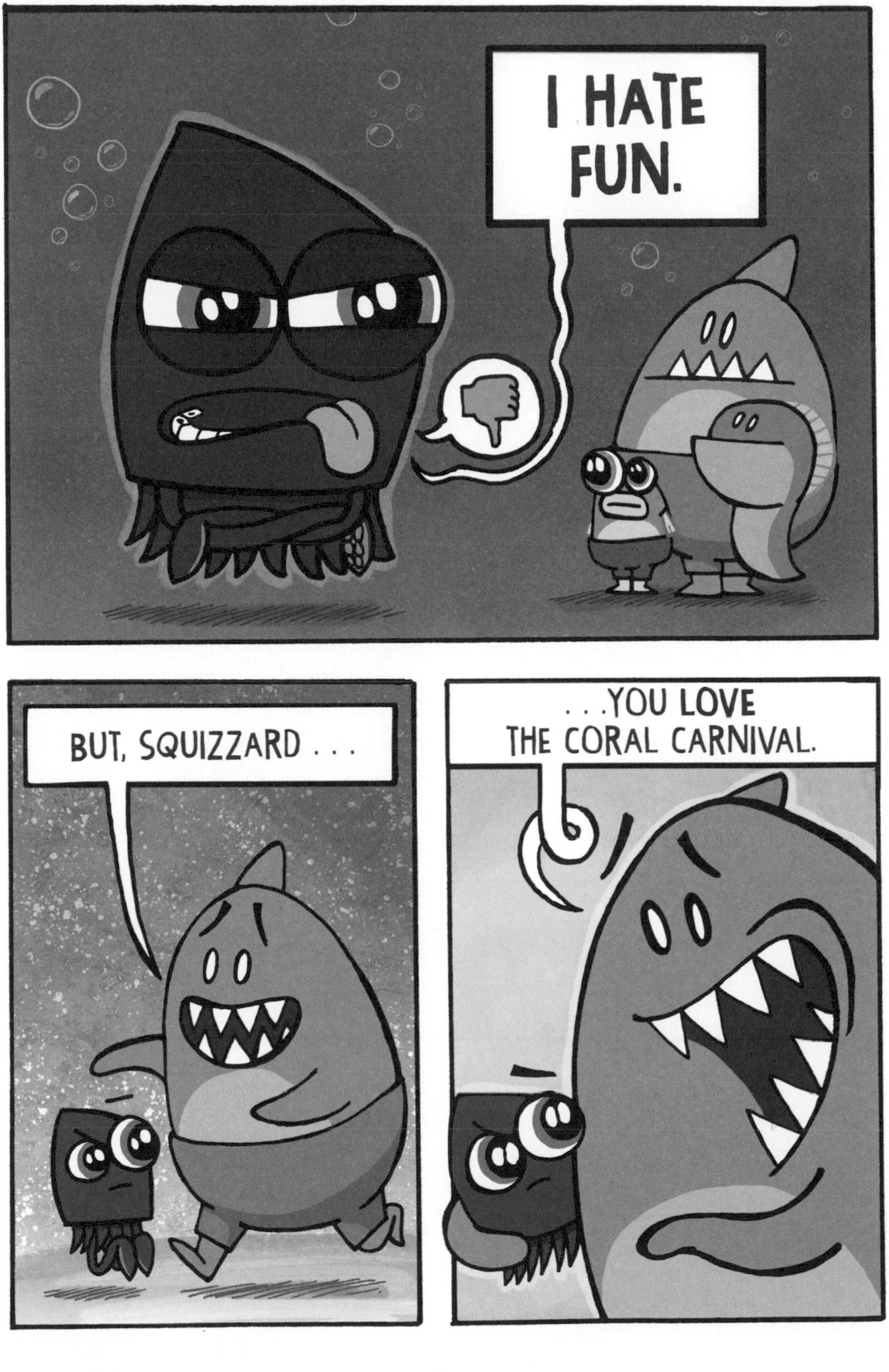
I HATE FUN.
BUT, SQUIZZARD . . .
. . .YOU LOVE THE CORAL CARNIVAL.

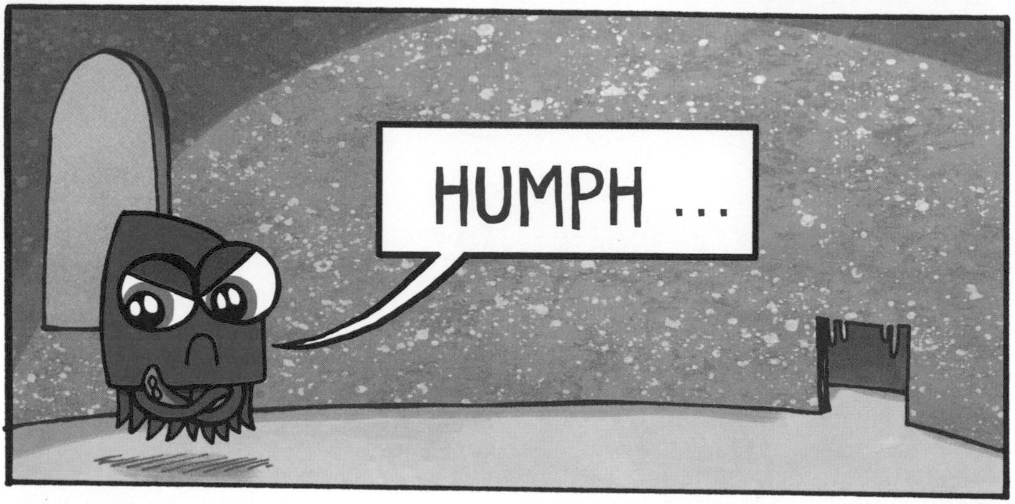
HUMPH ...

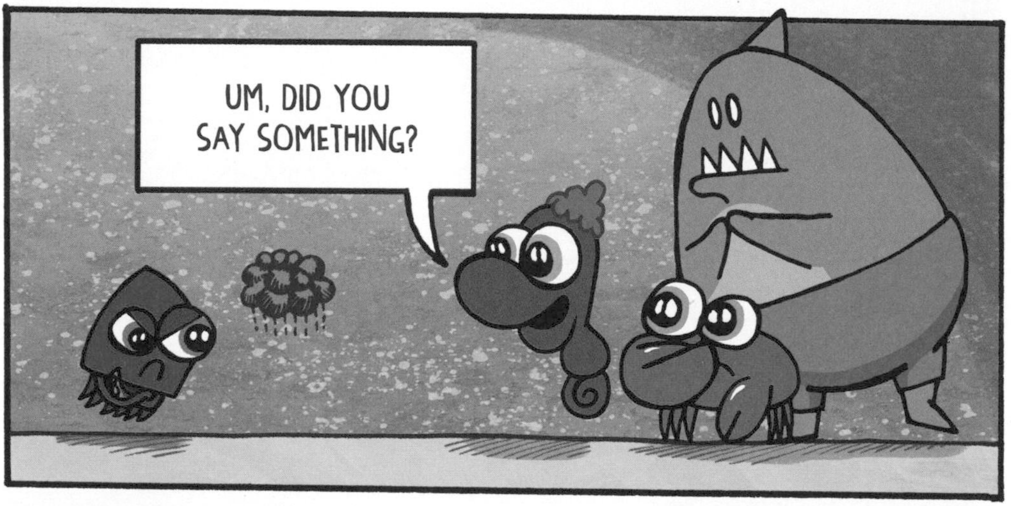
UM, DID YOU SAY SOMETHING?

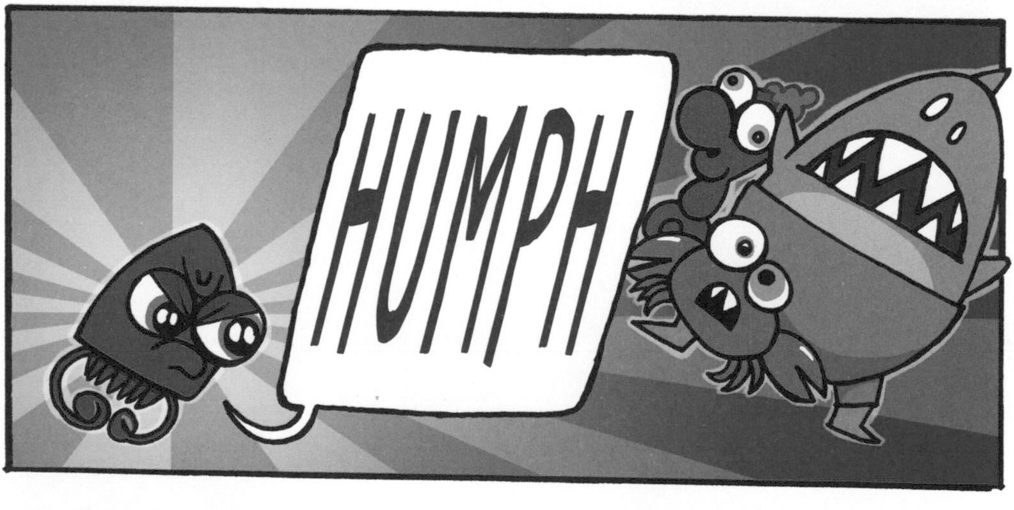
HUMPH

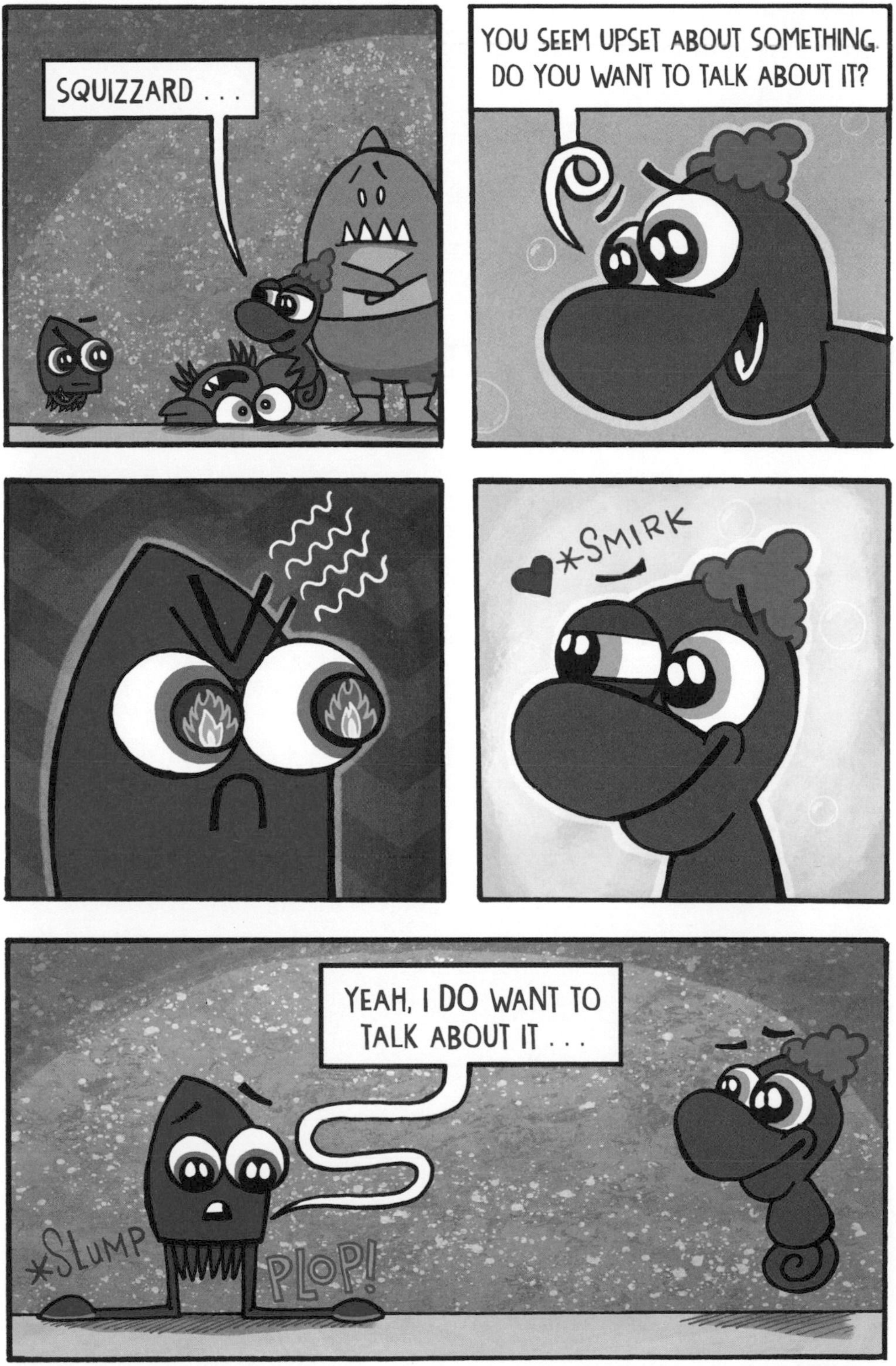
SQUIZZARD . . .
YOU SEEM UPSET ABOUT SOMETHING. DO YOU WANT TO TALK ABOUT IT?
*SMIRK
YEAH, I DO WANT TO TALK ABOUT IT . . .
*SLUMP
PLOP!

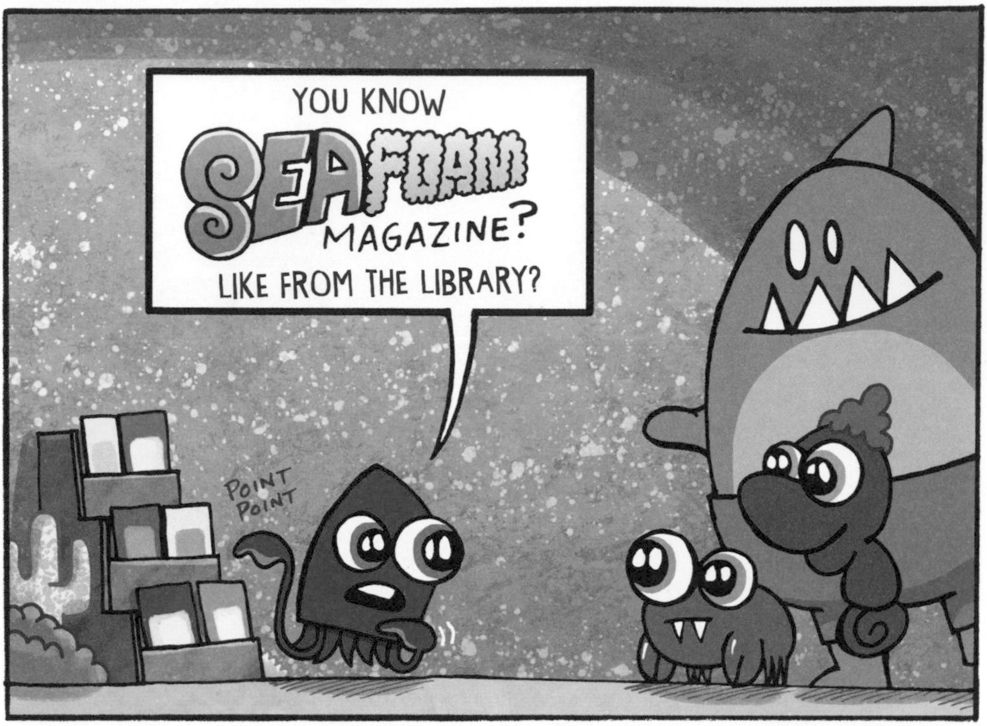
YOU KNOW SEAFOAM MAGAZINE? LIKE FROM THE LIBRARY?
POINT POINT

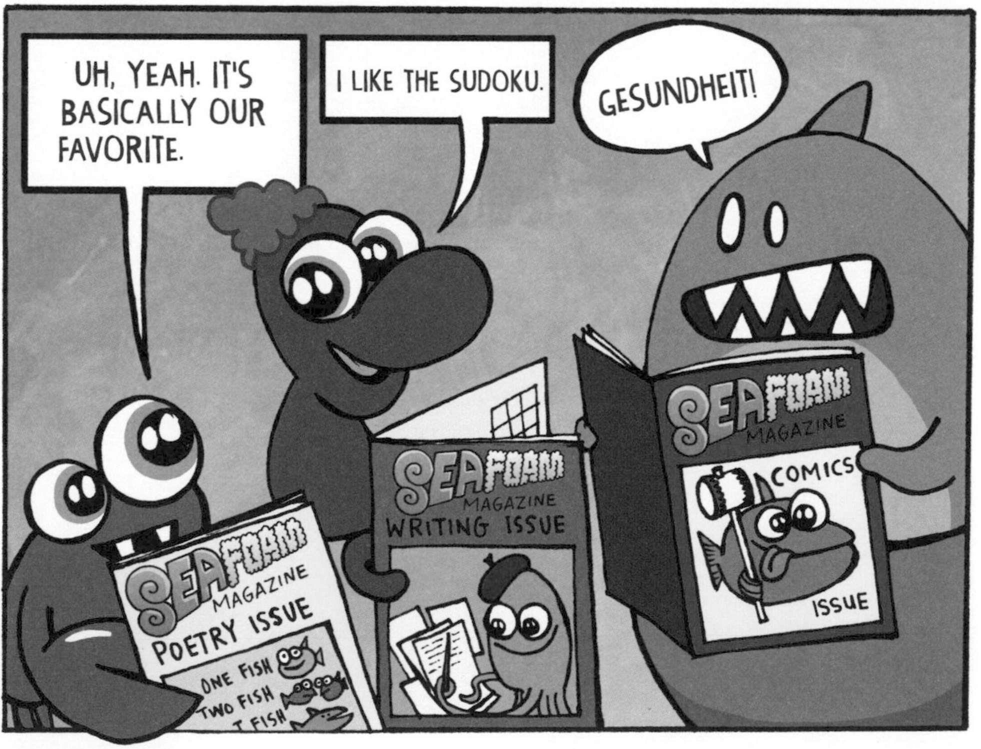
UH, YEAH. IT'S BASICALLY OUR FAVORITE.
I LIKE THE SUDOKU.
GESUNDHEIT!
SEAFOAM MAGAZINE POETRY ISSUE
ONE FISH TWO FISH
SEAFOAM MAGAZINE WRITING ISSUE
SEAFOAM MAGAZINE COMICS ISSUE

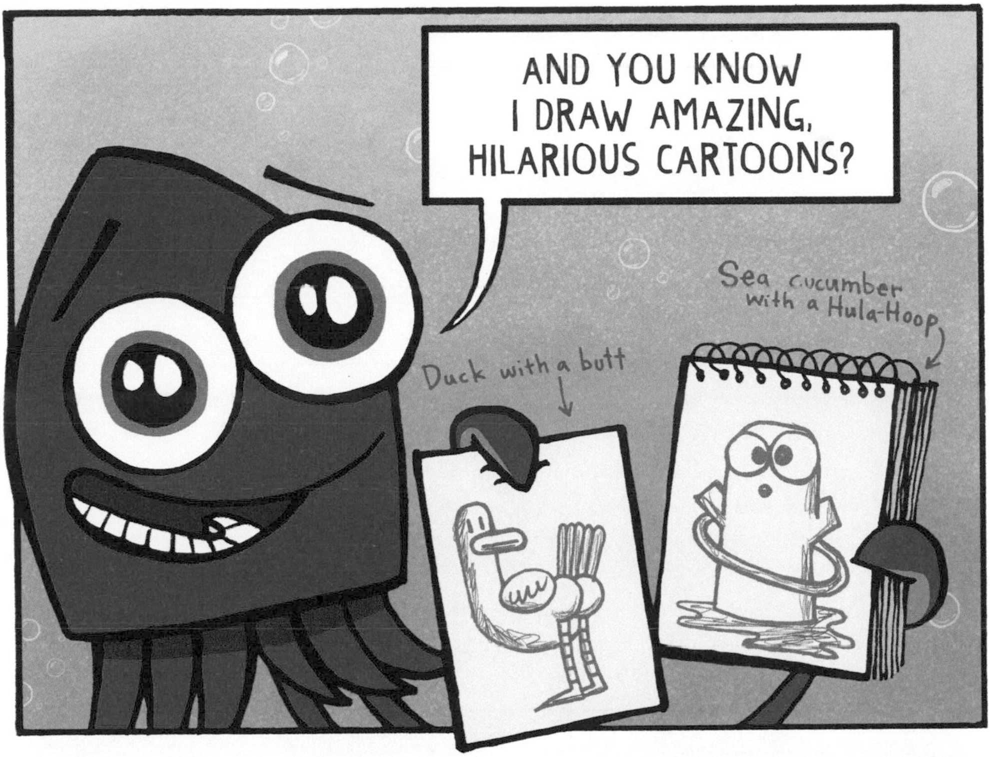
AND YOU KNOW I DRAW AMAZING, HILARIOUS CARTOONS?
Sea cucumber with a Hula-Hoop
Duck with a butt

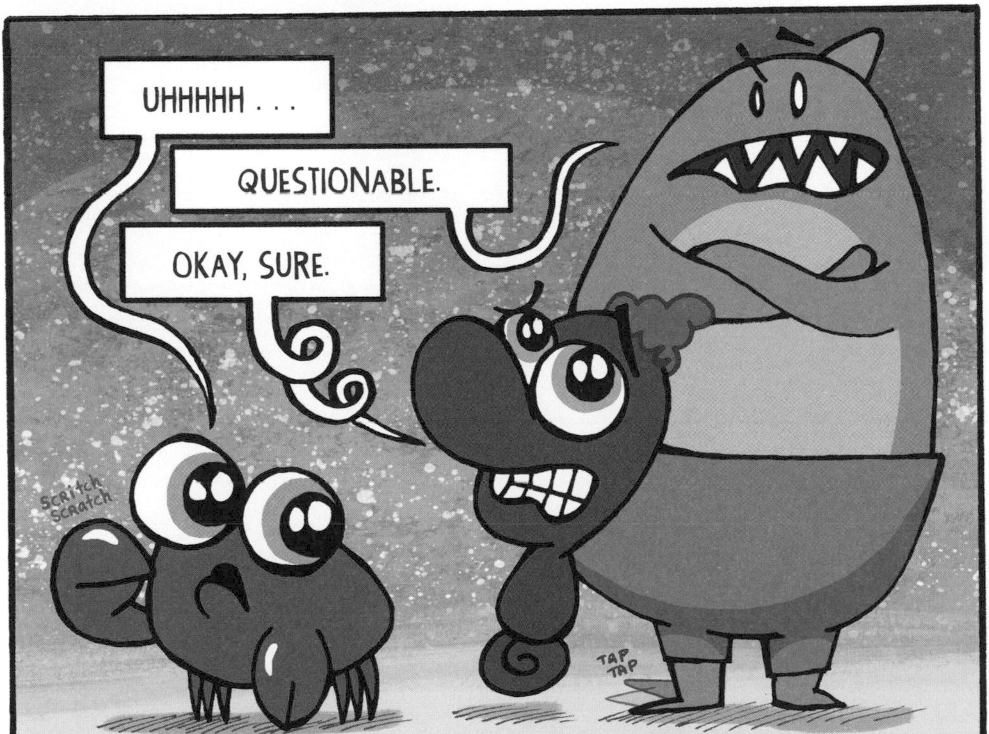
UHHHHH . . .
QUESTIONABLE.
OKAY, SURE.
SCRITCH SCRATCH
TAP TAP

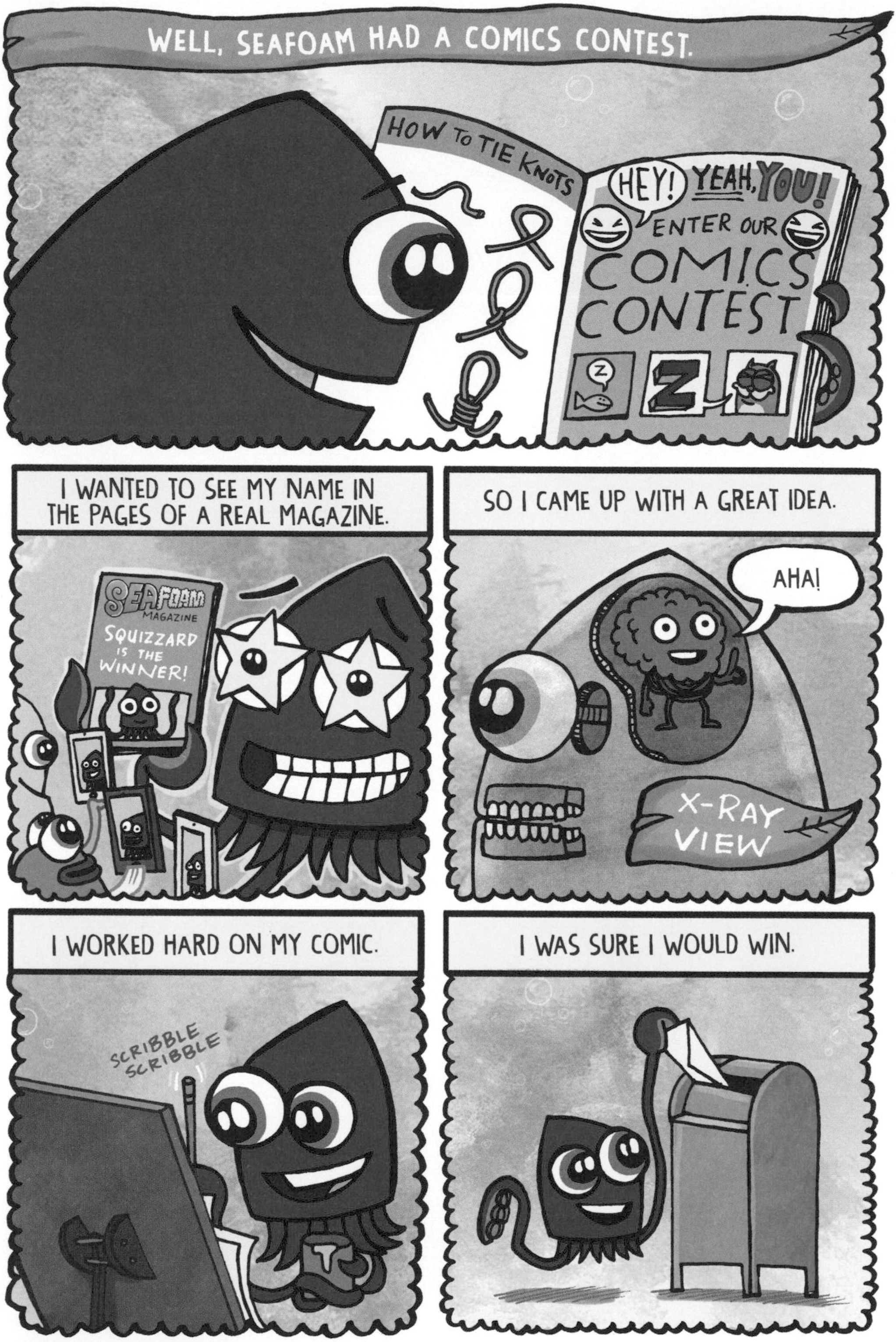
WELL, SEAFOAM HAD A COMICS CONTEST.
HOW TO TIE KNOTS
HEY! YEAH, YOU!
ENTER OUR
COMICS CONTEST
Z
I WANTED TO SEE MY NAME IN THE PAGES OF A REAL MAGAZINE.
SEAFOAM MAGAZINE
SQUIZZARD IS THE WINNER!
SO I CAME UP WITH A GREAT IDEA.
AHA!
X-RAY VIEW
I WORKED HARD ON MY COMIC.
SCRIBBLE SCRIBBLE
I WAS SURE I WOULD WIN.

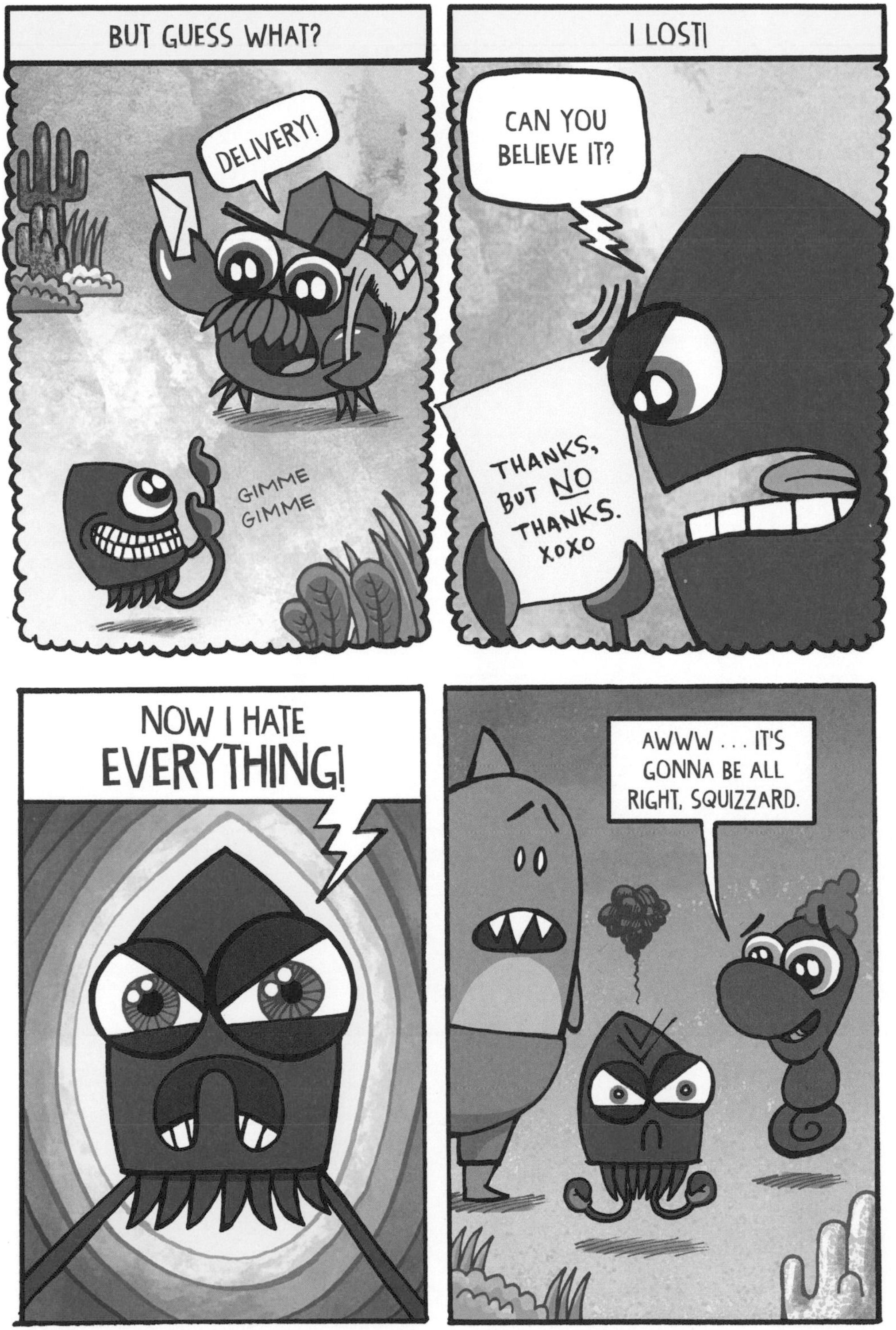
BUT GUESS WHAT?
DELIVERY!
GIMME
GIMME
I LOST!
CAN YOU BELIEVE IT?
THANKS, BUT NO THANKS. XOXO
NOW I HATE EVERYTHING!
AWWW . . . IT'S GONNA BE ALL RIGHT, SQUIZZARD.

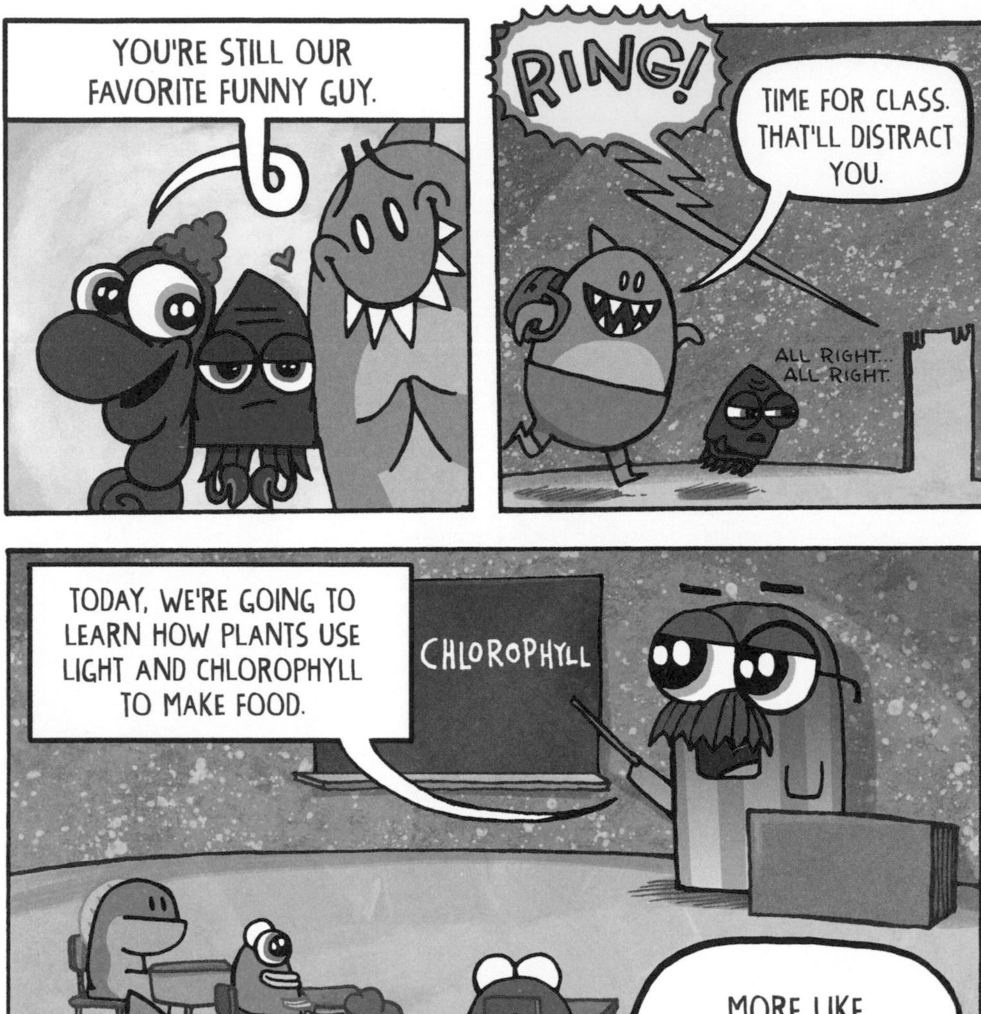

YOU'RE STILL OUR FAVORITE FUNNY GUY.
RING!
TIME FOR CLASS. THAT'LL DISTRACT YOU.
ALL RIGHT... ALL RIGHT.
TODAY, WE'RE GOING TO LEARN HOW PLANTS USE LIGHT AND CHLOROPHYLL TO MAKE FOOD.
CHLOROPHYLL
MORE LIKE BORE-O-FILL!
SHHHH!
SOMEONE IS SALTY!
HEH HEH...

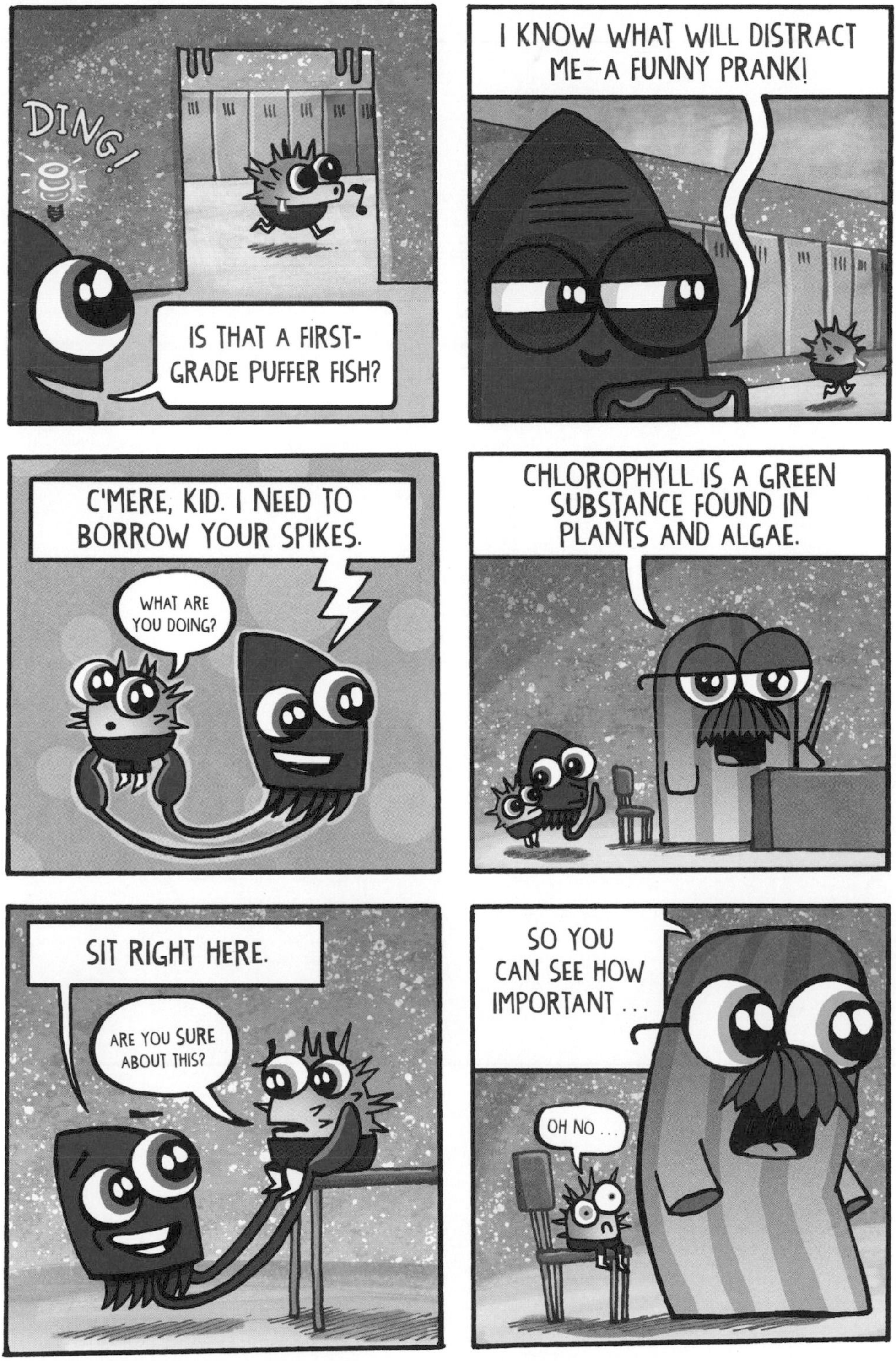
DING!
IS THAT A FIRST-GRADE PUFFER FISH?
I KNOW WHAT WILL DISTRACT ME—A FUNNY PRANK!
C'MERE, KID. I NEED TO BORROW YOUR SPIKES.
WHAT ARE YOU DOING?
CHLOROPHYLL IS A GREEN SUBSTANCE FOUND IN PLANTS AND ALGAE.
SIT RIGHT HERE.
ARE YOU SURE ABOUT THIS?
SO YOU CAN SEE HOW IMPORTANT . . .
OH NO . . .

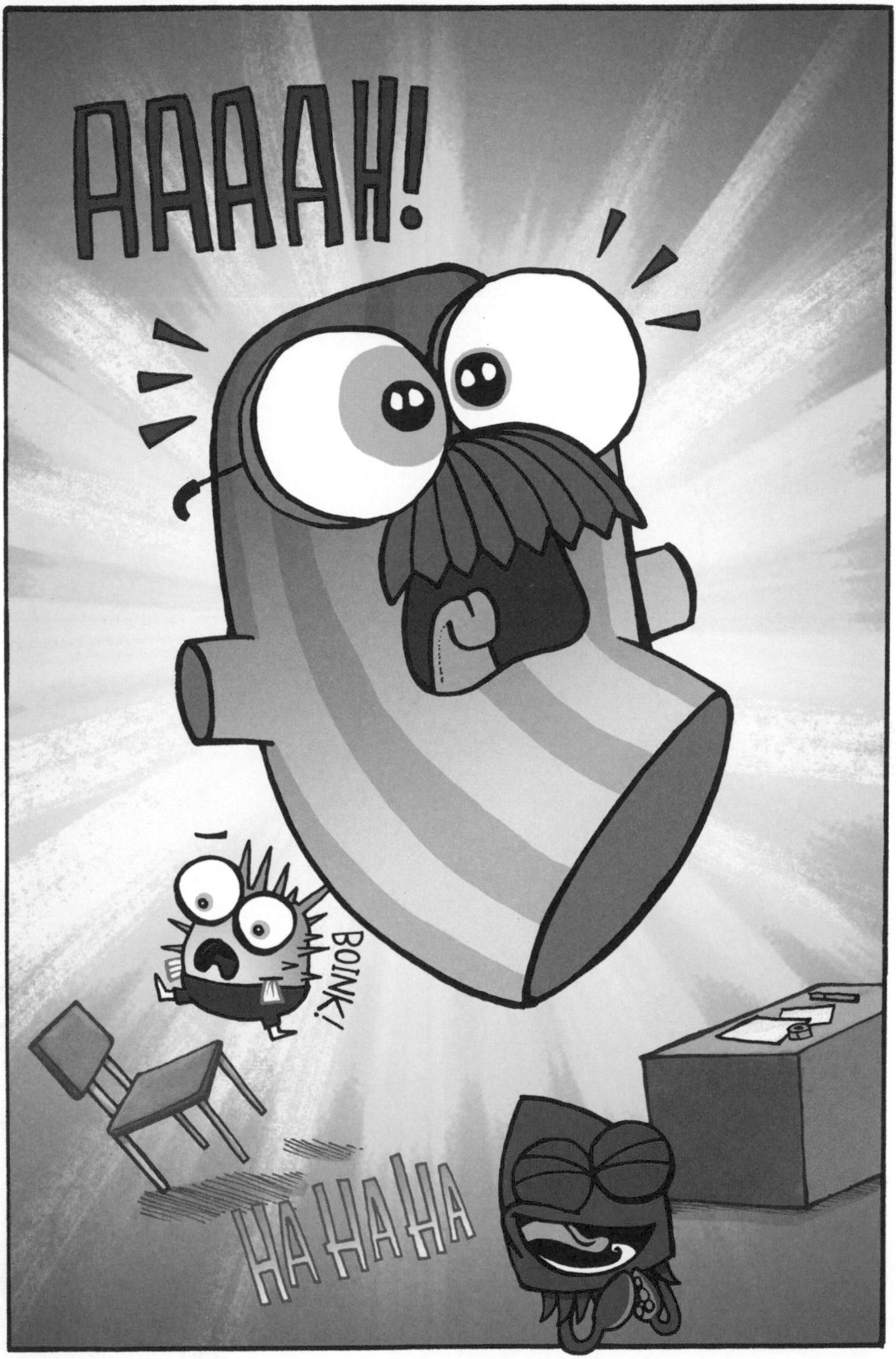
AAAAH!
BOIINK!
HA HA HA HA

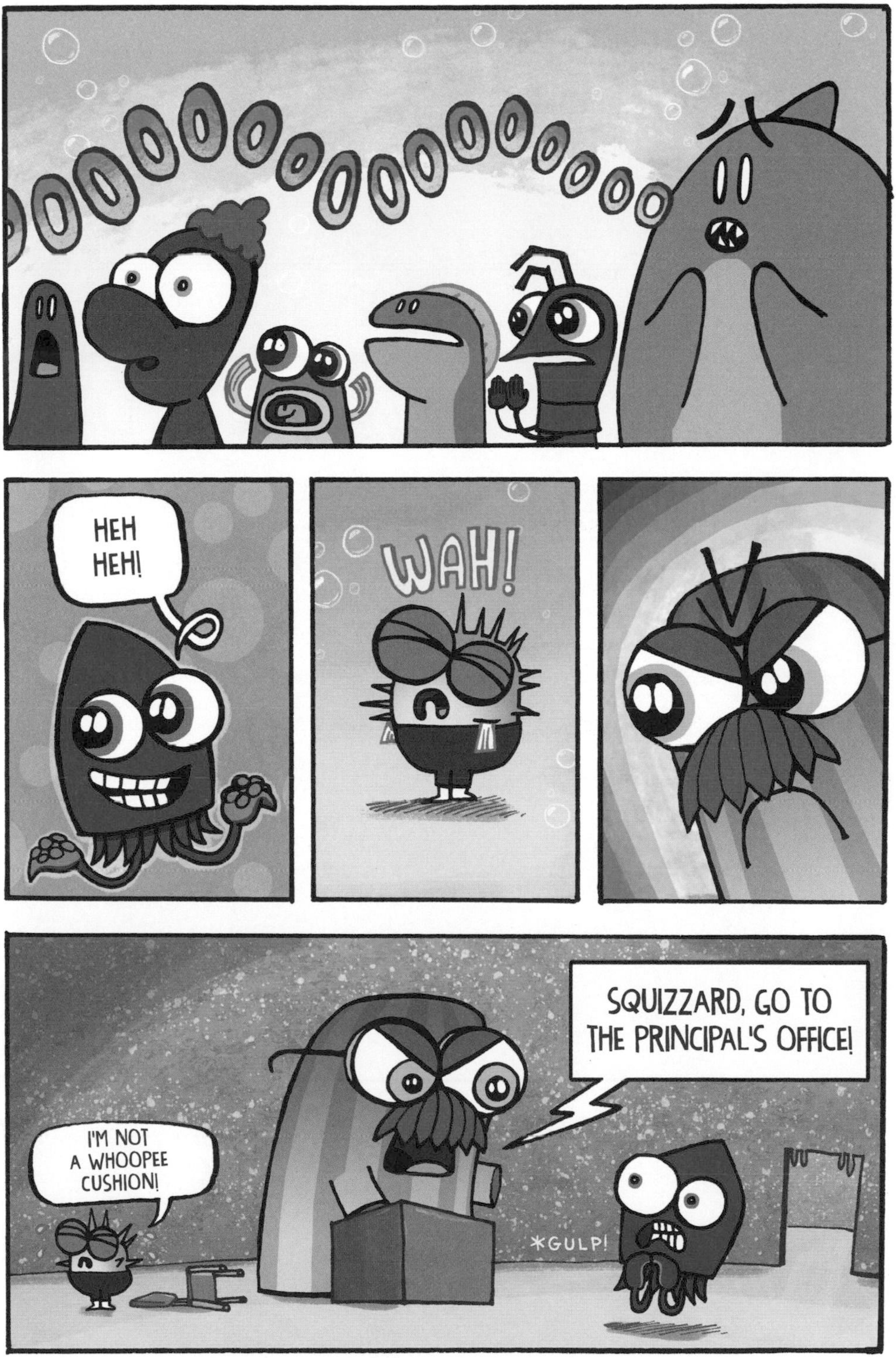
OOOOOOOOOOOOOOOOOOOO
HEH HEH!
WAH!
I'M NOT A WHOOPEE CUSHION!
SQUIZZARD, GO TO THE PRINCIPAL'S OFFICE!
*GULP!

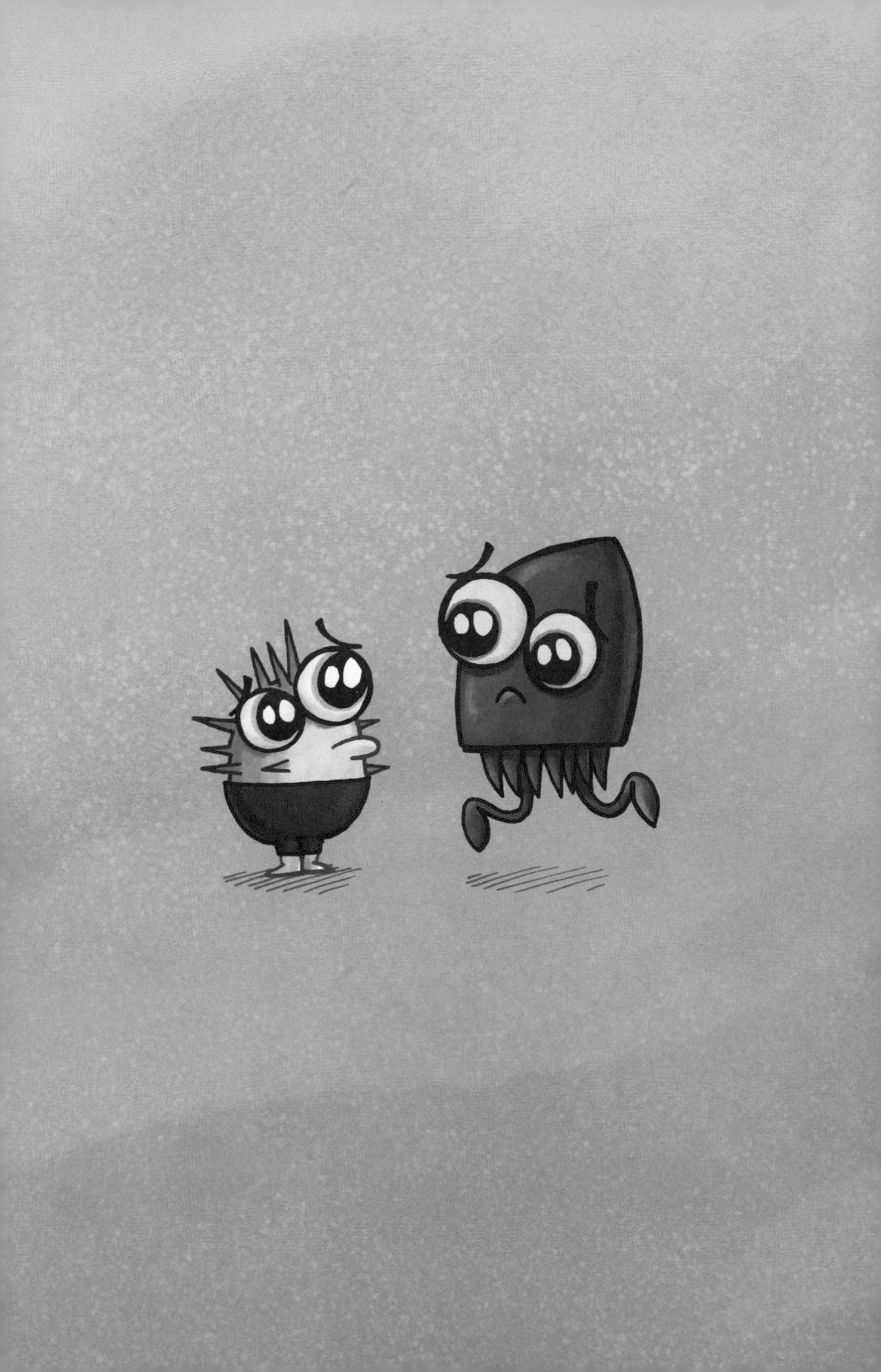

CHAPTER 2

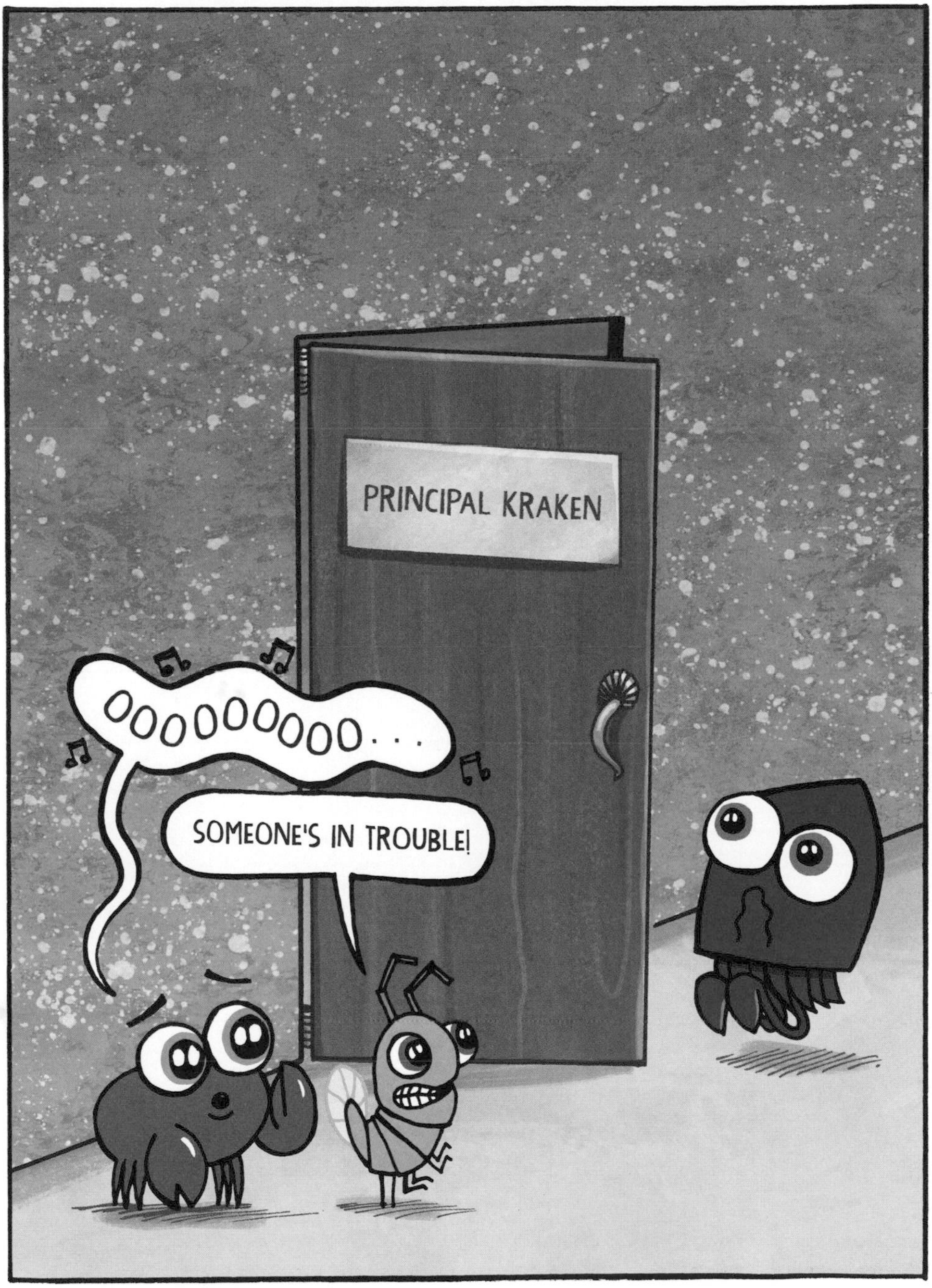
PRINCIPAL KRAKEN
OOOOOOOOOO. . .
SOMEONE'S IN TROUBLE!

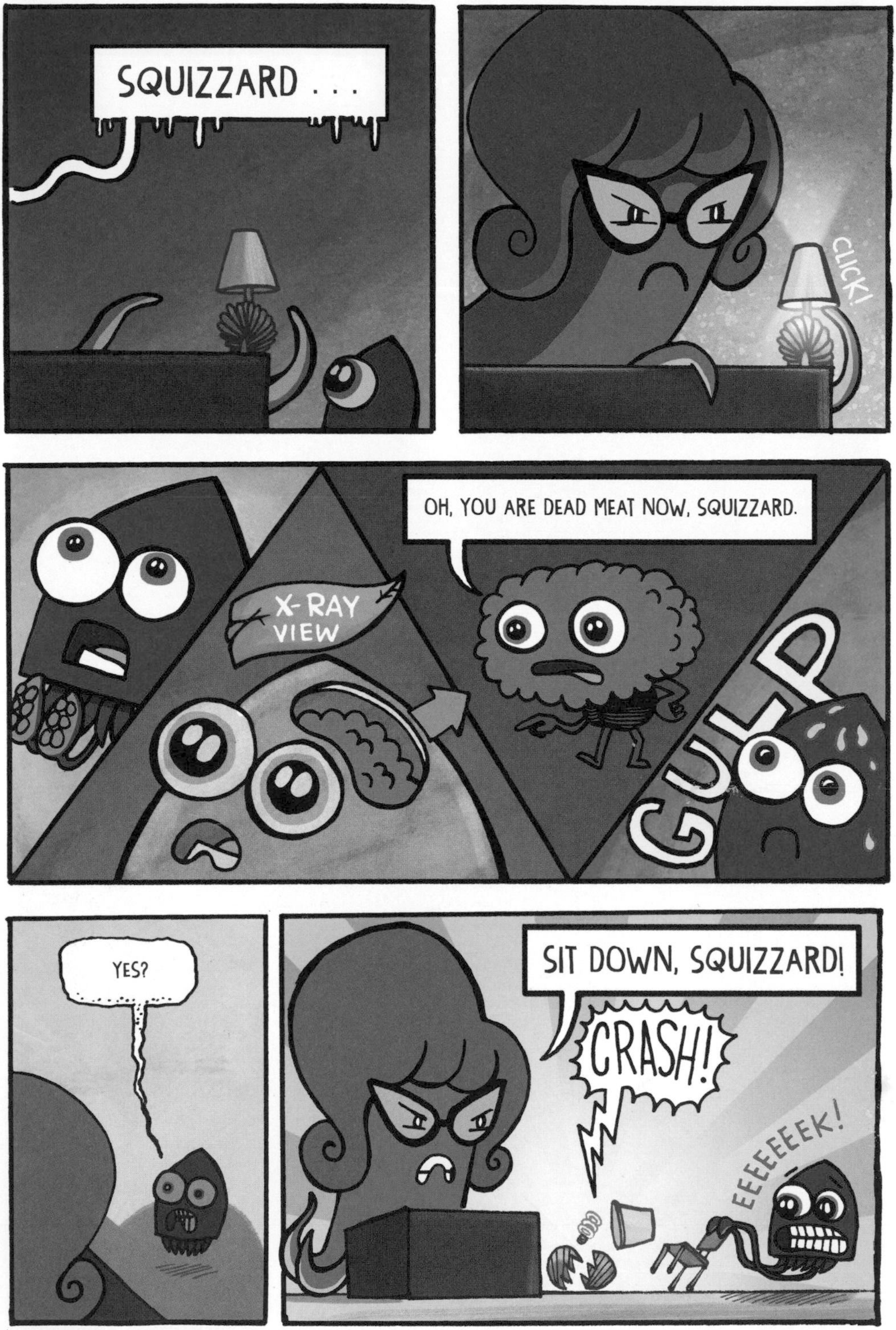
SQUIZZARD . . .
CLICK!
X-RAY VIEW
OH, YOU ARE DEAD MEAT NOW, SQUIZZARD.
GULP
YES?
SIT DOWN, SQUIZZARD!
CRASH!
EEEEEEEK!

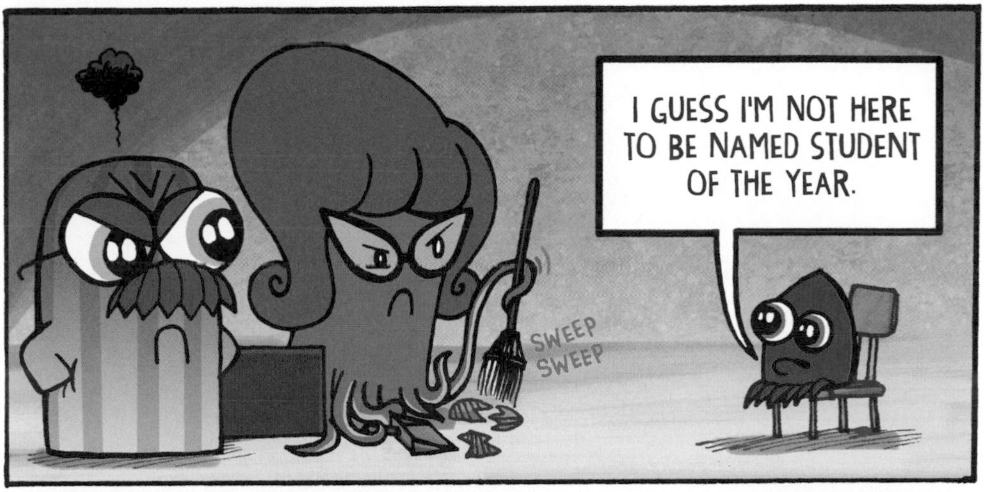
I GUESS I'M NOT HERE TO BE NAMED STUDENT OF THE YEAR.
SWEEP SWEEP

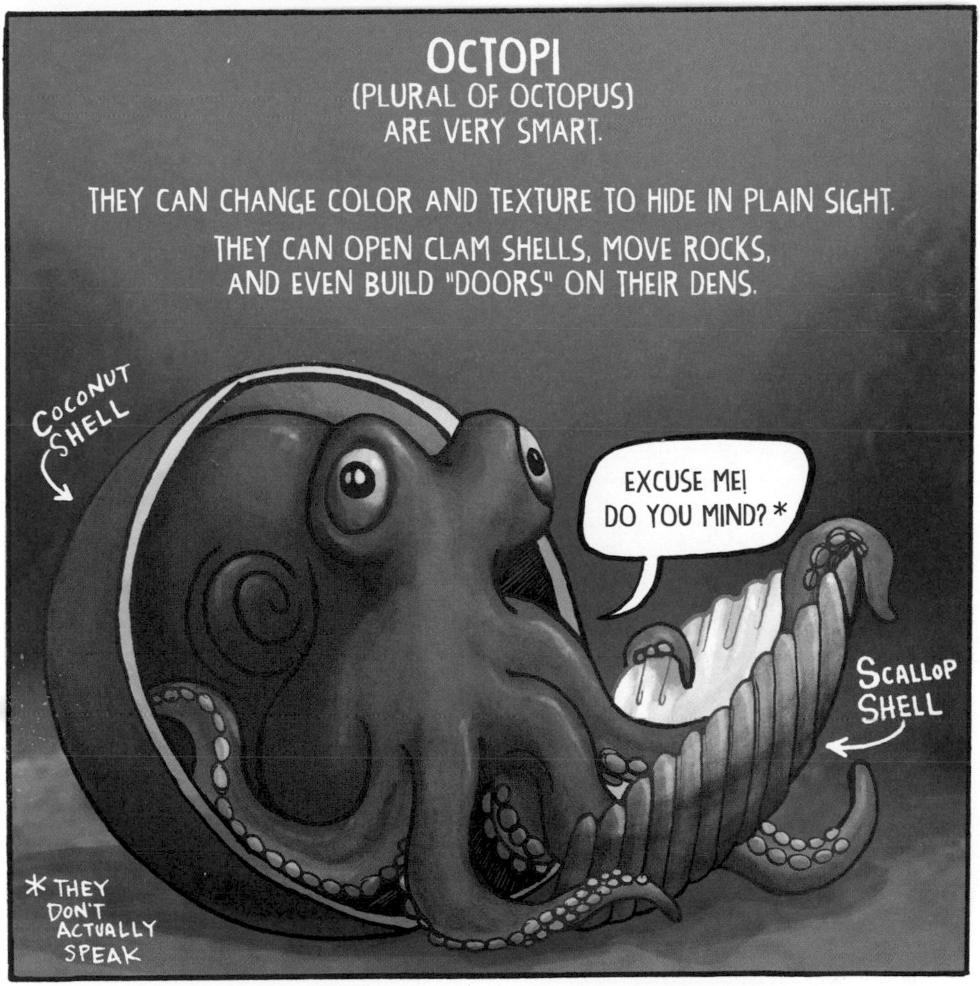
OCTOPI
(PLURAL OF OCTOPUS)
ARE VERY SMART.
THEY CAN CHANGE COLOR AND TEXTURE TO HIDE IN PLAIN SIGHT.
THEY CAN OPEN CLAM SHELLS, MOVE ROCKS, AND EVEN BUILD "DOORS" ON THEIR DENS.
COCONUT SHELL
EXCUSE ME! DO YOU MIND? *
SCALLOP SHELL
* THEY DON'T ACTUALLY SPEAK

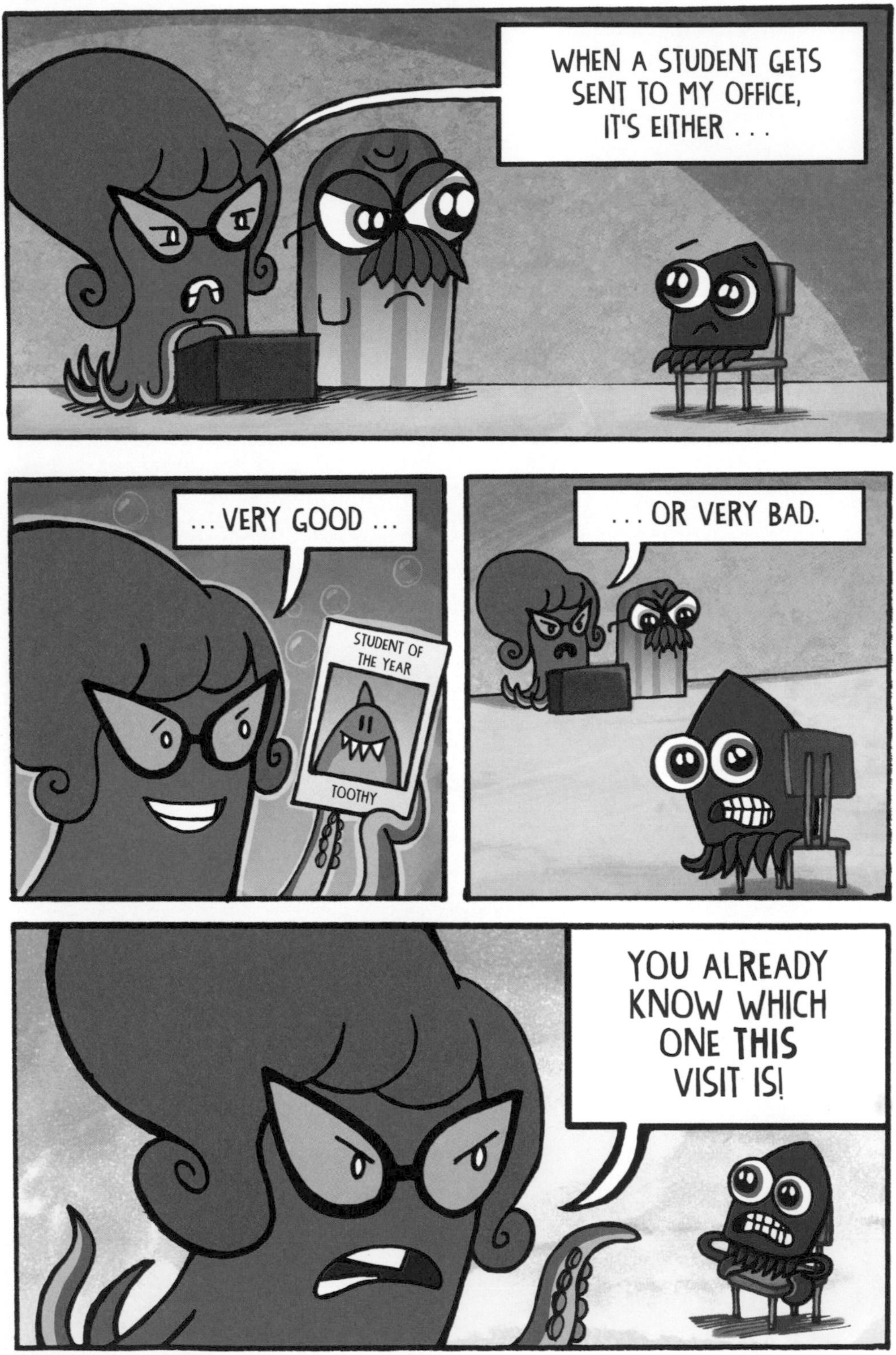
WHEN A STUDENT GETS SENT TO MY OFFICE, IT'S EITHER . . .
... VERY GOOD ...
STUDENT OF THE YEAR
TOOTHY
. . . OR VERY BAD.
YOU ALREADY KNOW WHICH ONE THIS VISIT IS!

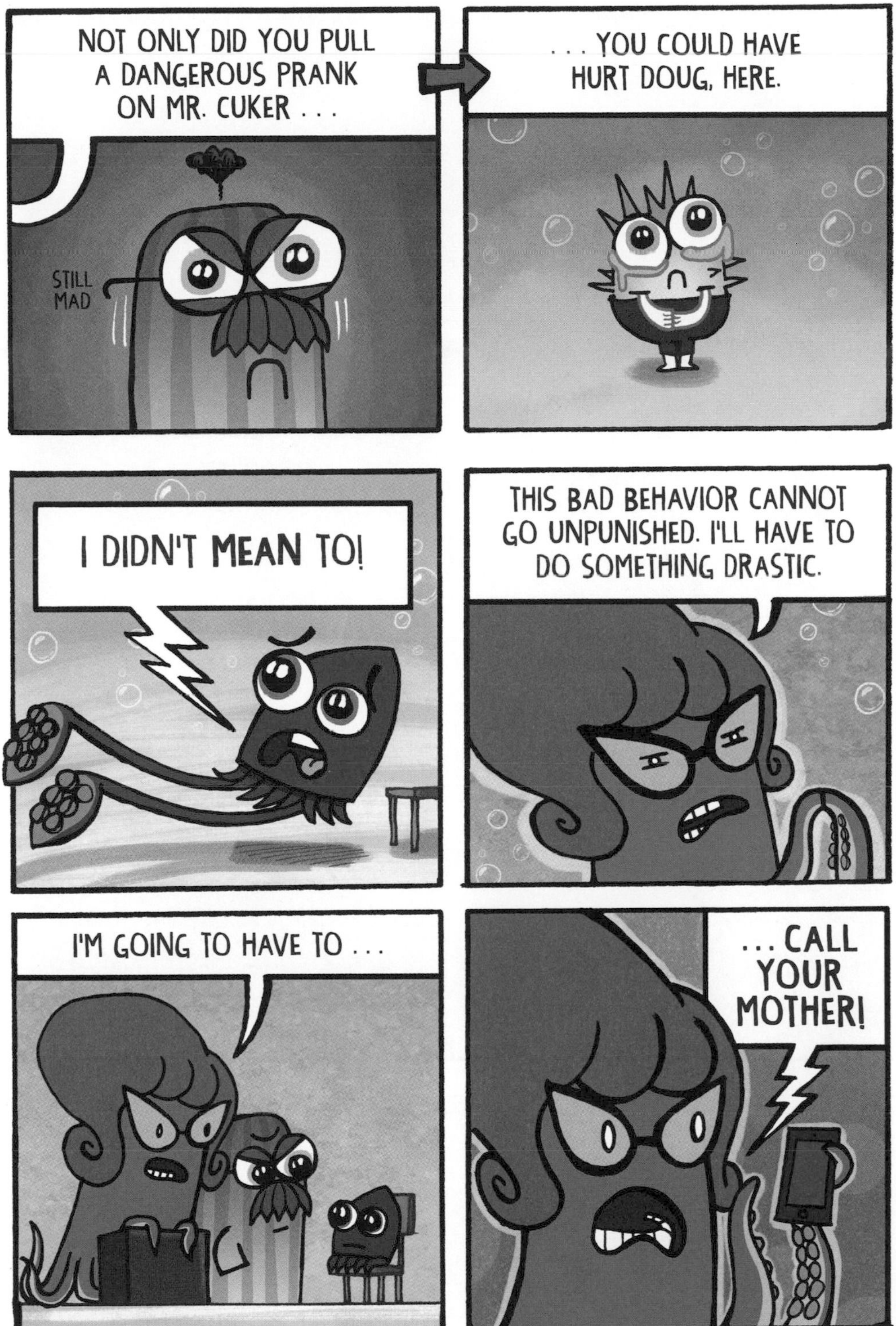
NOT ONLY DID YOU PULL A DANGEROUS PRANK ON MR. CUKER . . .
STILL MAD
. . . YOU COULD HAVE HURT DOUG, HERE.
I DIDN'T MEAN TO!
THIS BAD BEHAVIOR CANNOT GO UNPUNISHED. I'LL HAVE TO DO SOMETHING DRASTIC.
I'M GOING TO HAVE TO . . .
. . . CALL YOUR MOTHER!

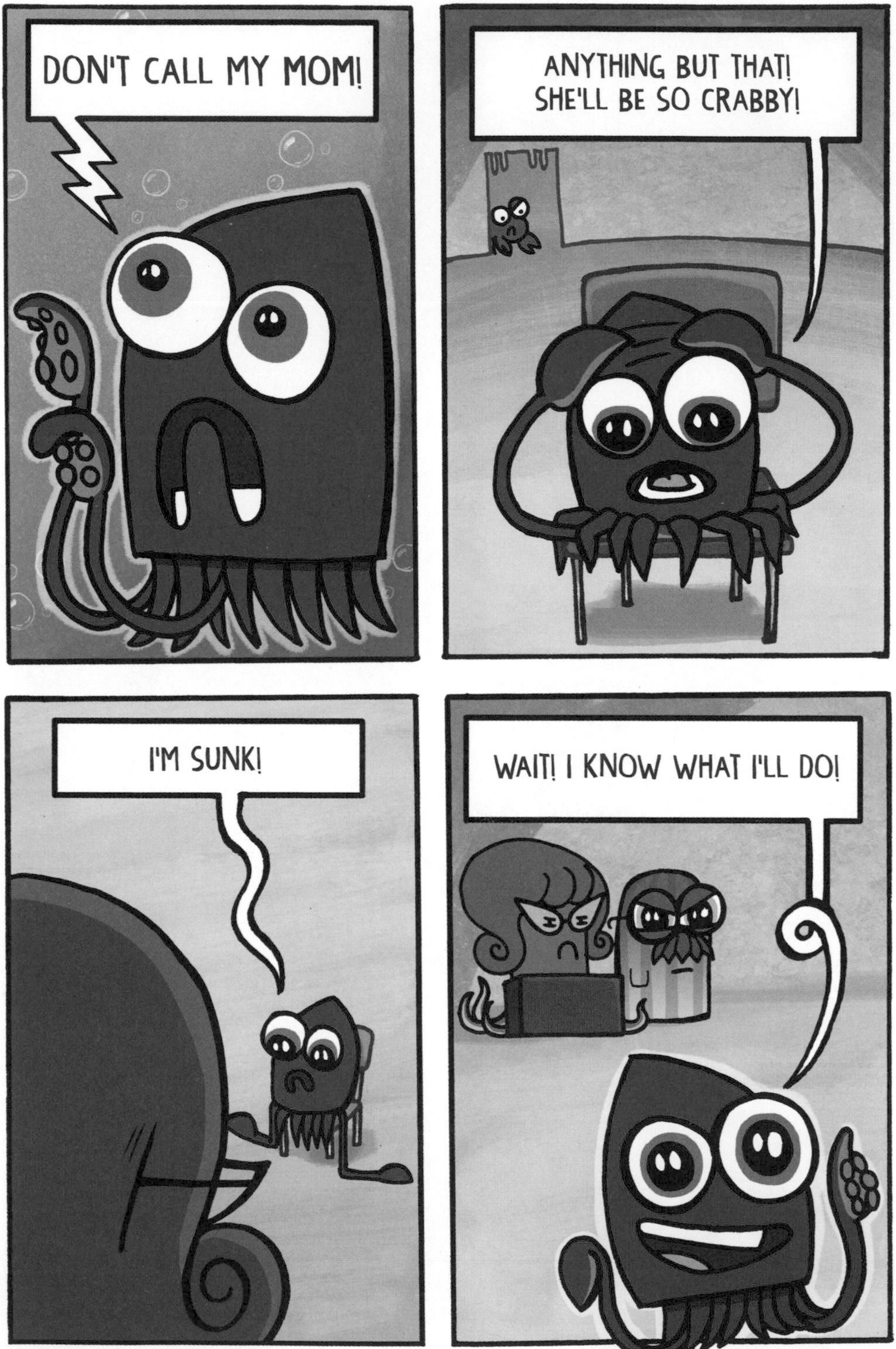
DON'T CALL MY MOM!
ANYTHING BUT THAT! SHE'LL BE SO CRABBY!
I'M SUNK!
WAIT! I KNOW WHAT I'LL DO!

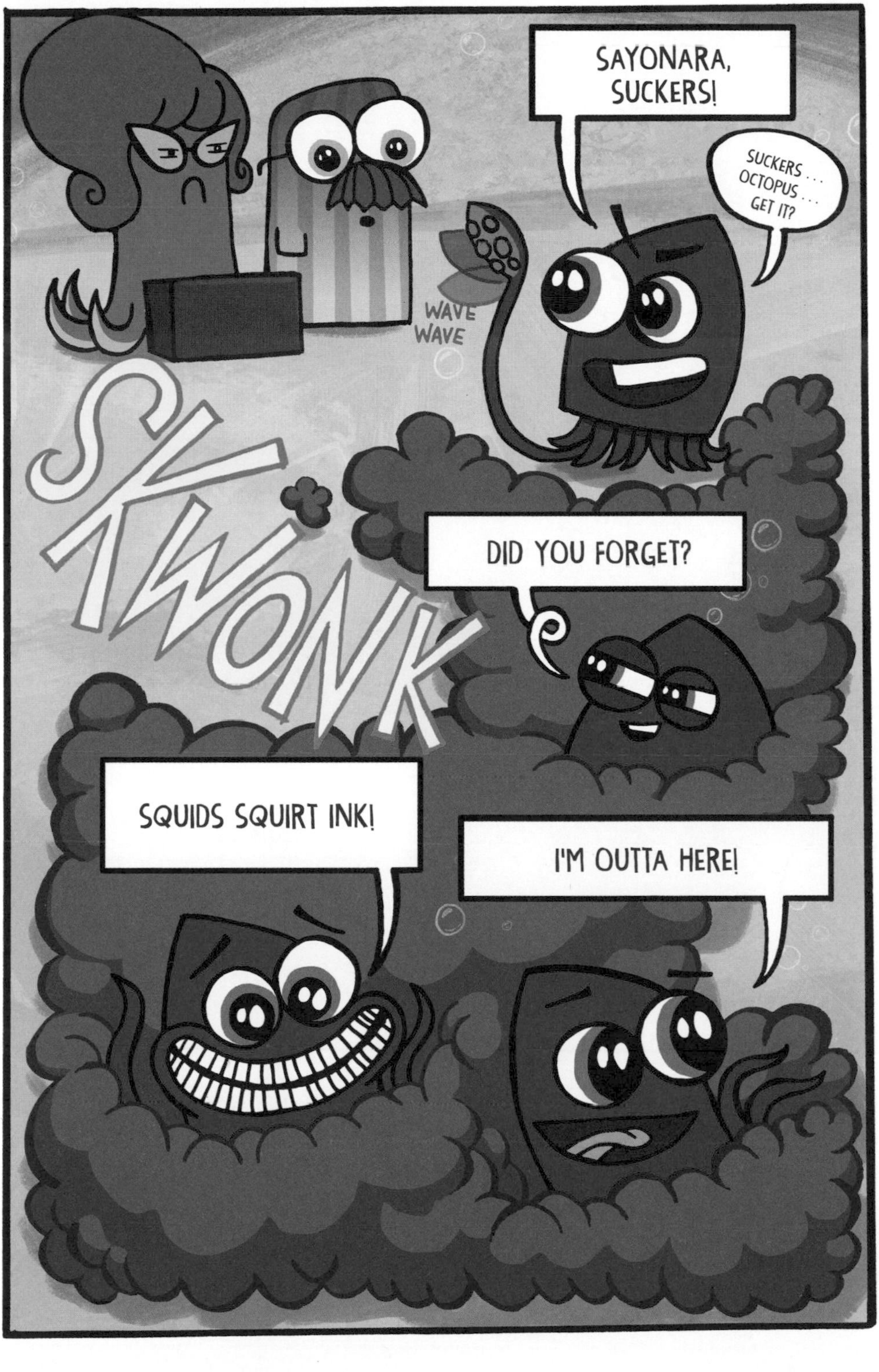
SAYONARA, SUCKERS!
SUCKERS . . . OCTOPUS . . . GET IT?
WAVE WAVE
SKWONK
DID YOU FORGET?
SQUIDS SQUIRT INK!
I'M OUTTA HERE!

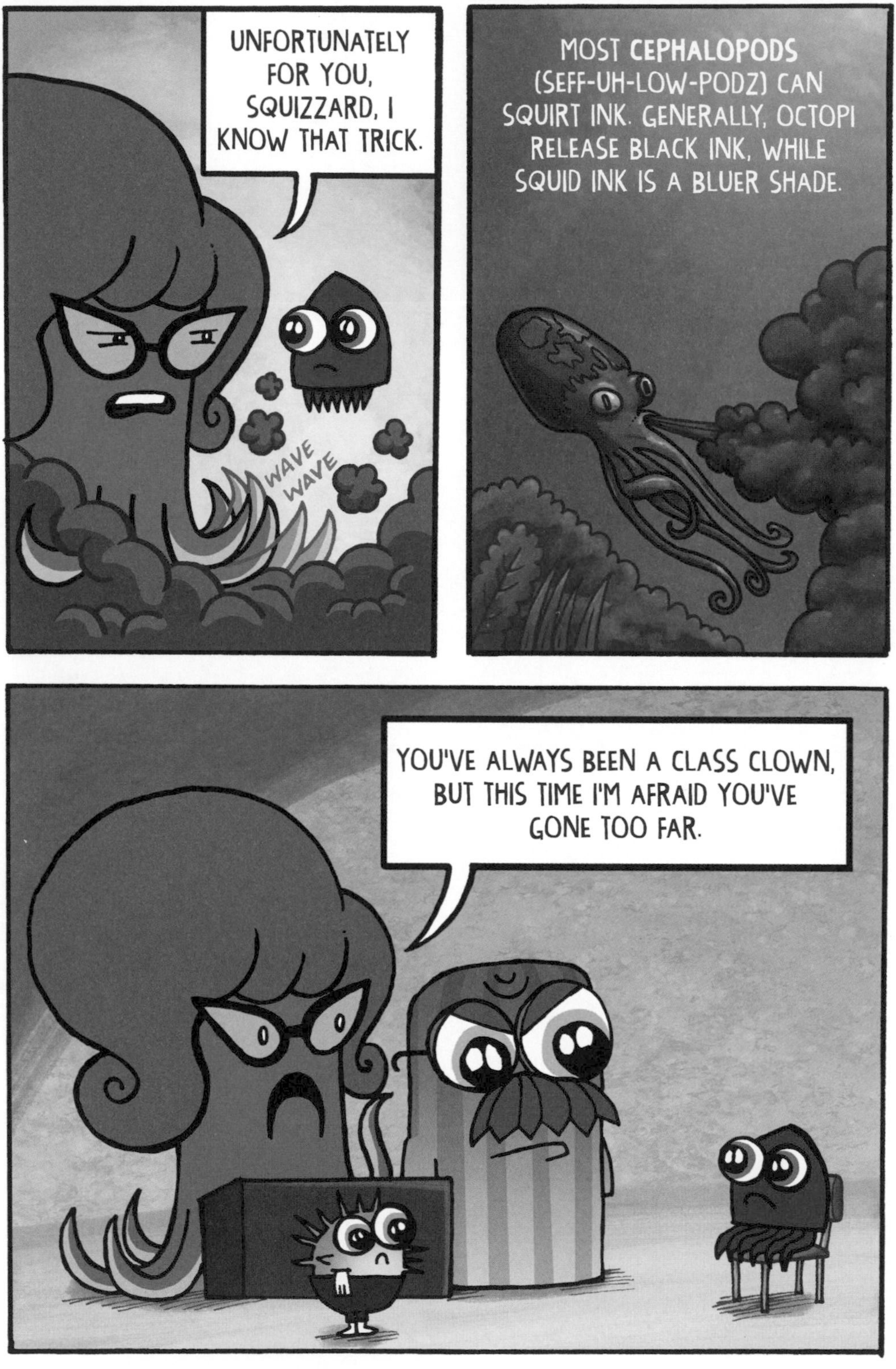
UNFORTUNATELY FOR YOU, SQUIZZARD, I KNOW THAT TRICK.
WAVE WAVE
MOST **CEPHALOPODS** (SEFF-UH-LOW-PODZ) CAN SQUIRT INK. GENERALLY, OCTOPI RELEASE BLACK INK, WHILE SQUID INK IS A BLUER SHADE.
YOU'VE ALWAYS BEEN A CLASS CLOWN, BUT THIS TIME I'M AFRAID YOU'VE GONE TOO FAR.

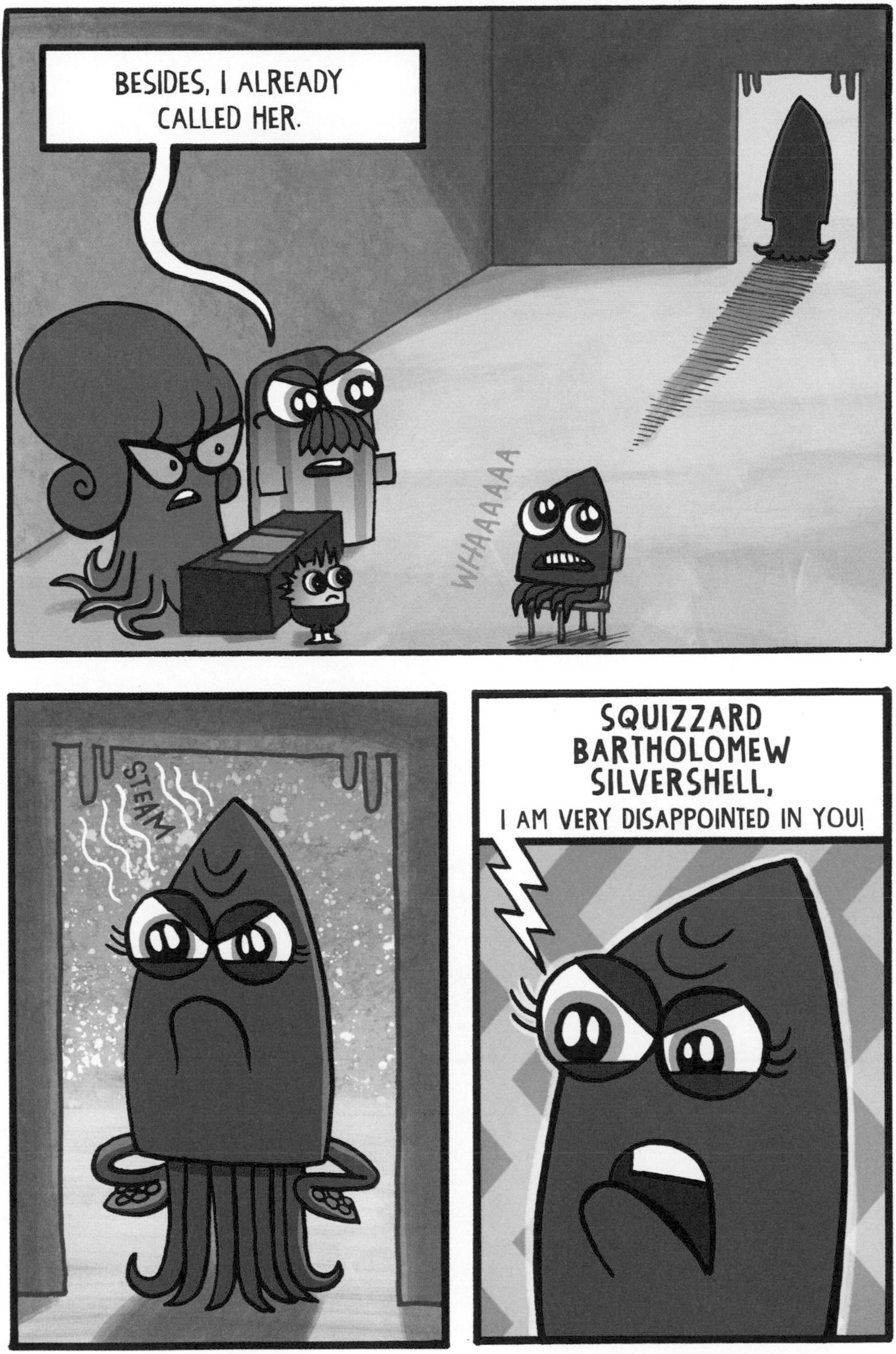
BESIDES, I ALREADY CALLED HER.
WHAAAAAA
STEAM
SQUIZZARD BARTHOLOMEW SILVERSHELL,
I AM VERY DISAPPOINTED IN YOU!

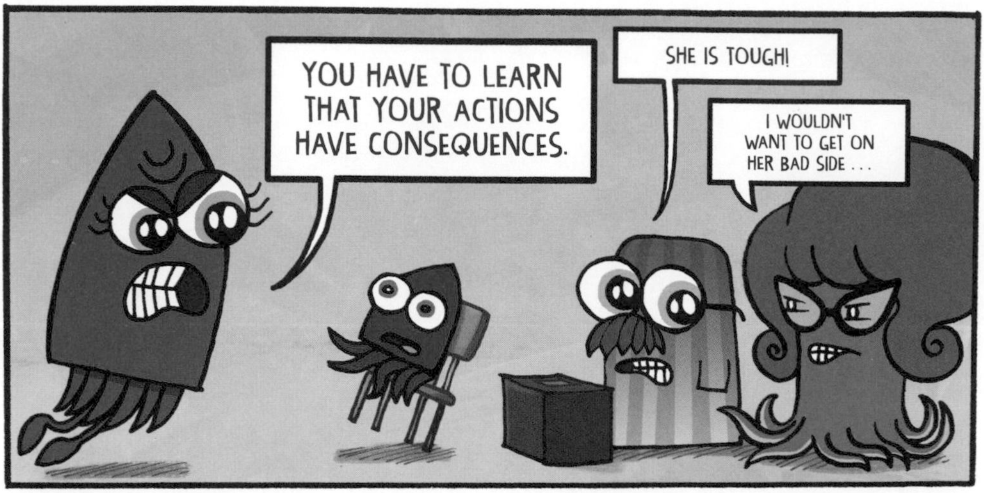
YOU HAVE TO LEARN THAT YOUR ACTIONS HAVE CONSEQUENCES.
SHE IS TOUGH!
I WOULDN'T WANT TO GET ON HER BAD SIDE . . .

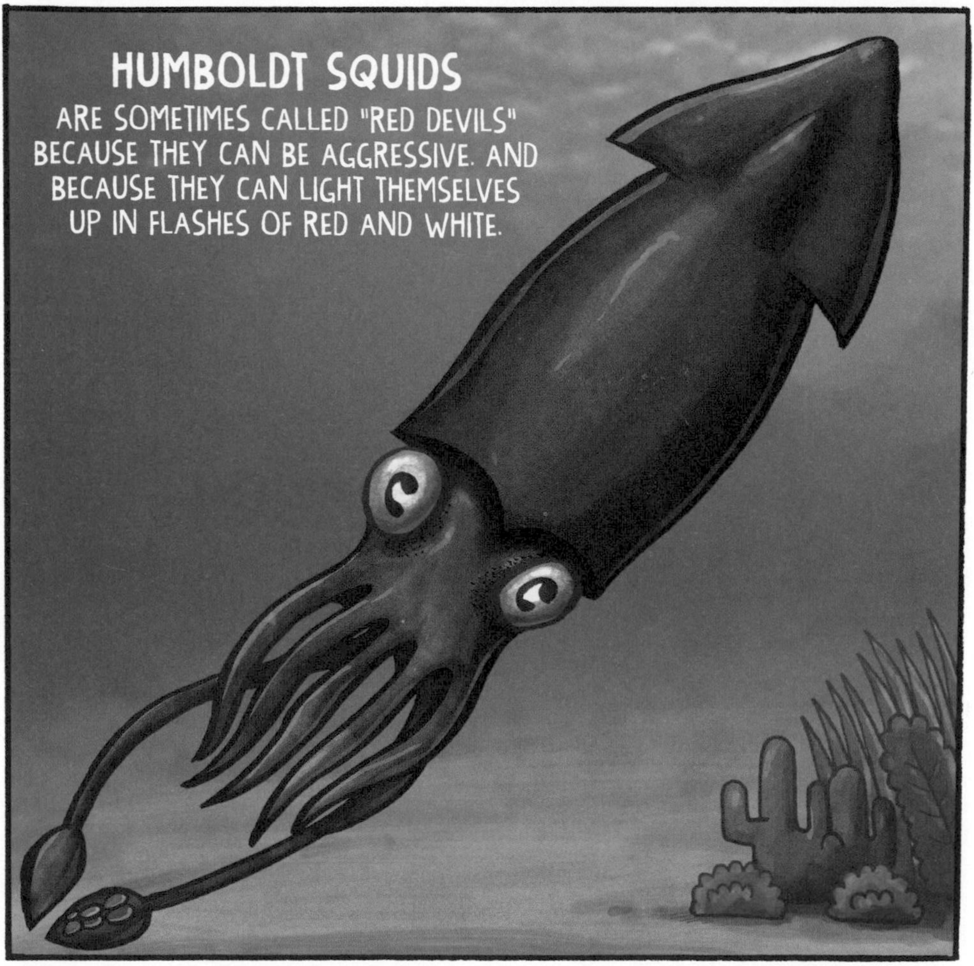
HUMBOLDT SQUIDS
ARE SOMETIMES CALLED "RED DEVILS" BECAUSE THEY CAN BE AGGRESSIVE. AND BECAUSE THEY CAN LIGHT THEMSELVES UP IN FLASHES OF RED AND WHITE.

27

CHAPTER 3

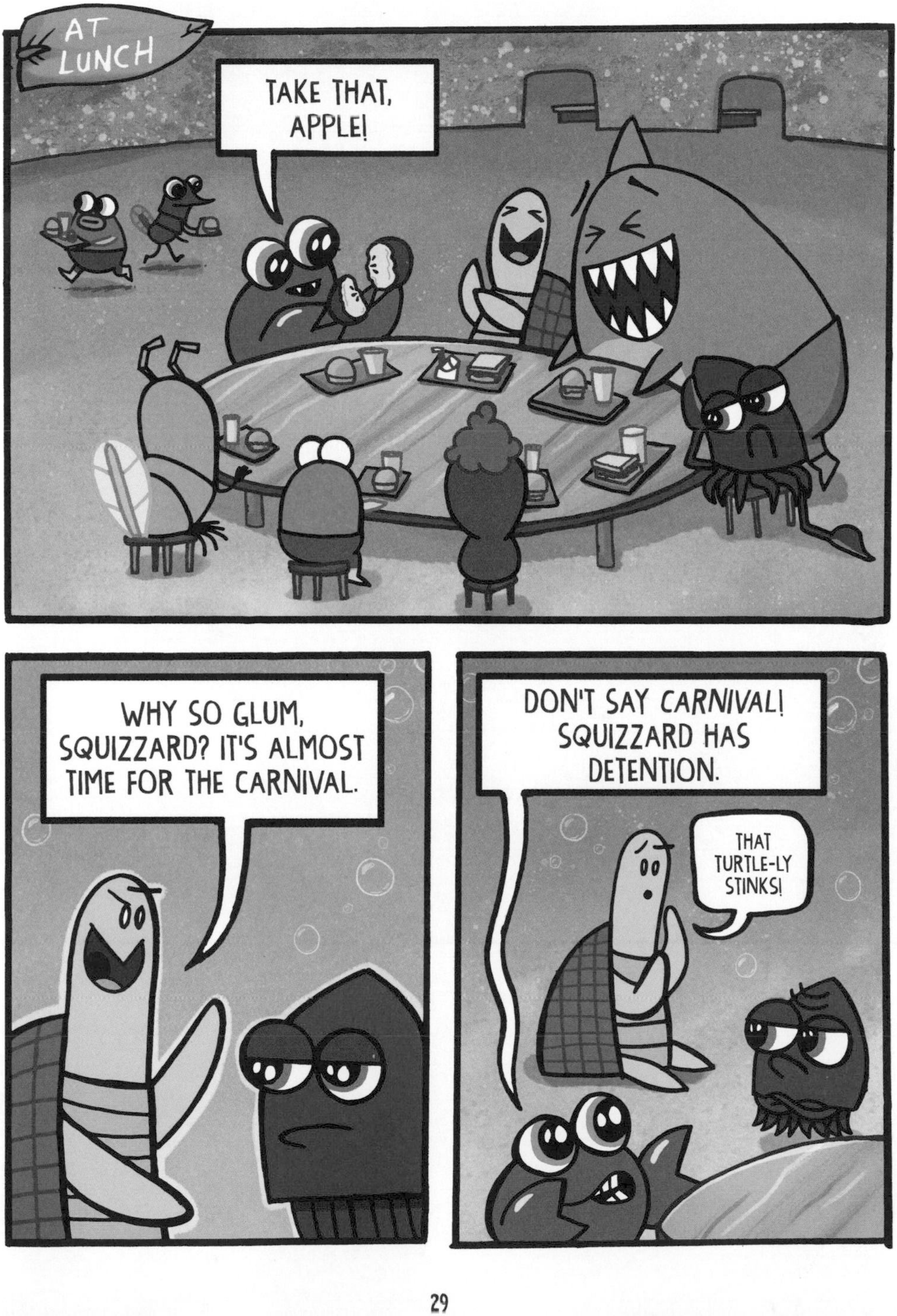
AT LUNCH
TAKE THAT, APPLE!
WHY SO GLUM, SQUIZZARD? IT'S ALMOST TIME FOR THE CARNIVAL.
DON'T SAY *CARNIVAL*! SQUIZZARD HAS DETENTION.
THAT TURTLE-LY STINKS!

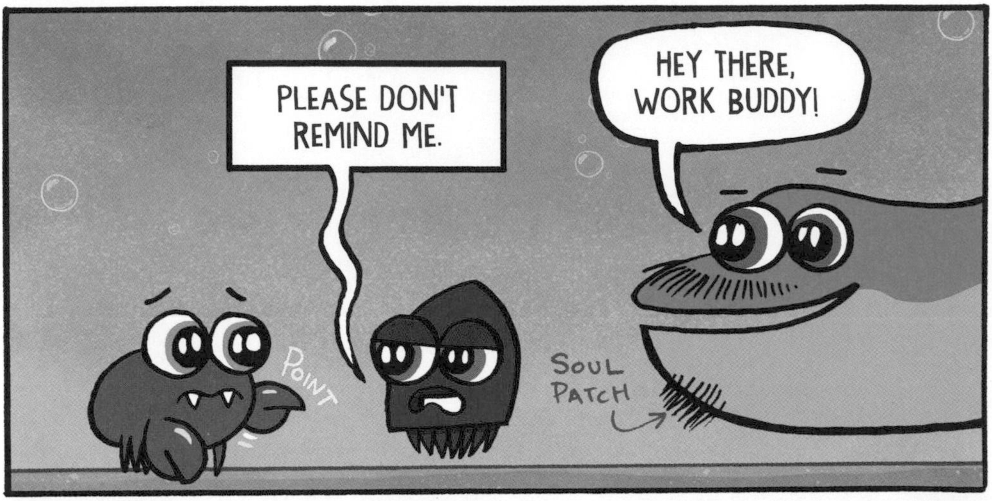
PLEASE DON'T REMIND ME.
HEY THERE, WORK BUDDY!
POINT
SOUL PATCH

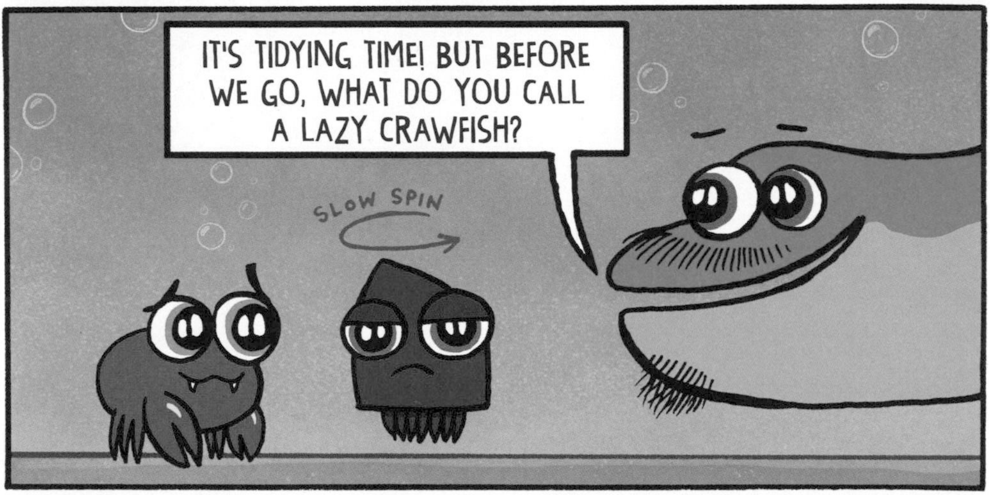
IT'S TIDYING TIME! BUT BEFORE WE GO, WHAT DO YOU CALL A LAZY CRAWFISH?
SLOW SPIN

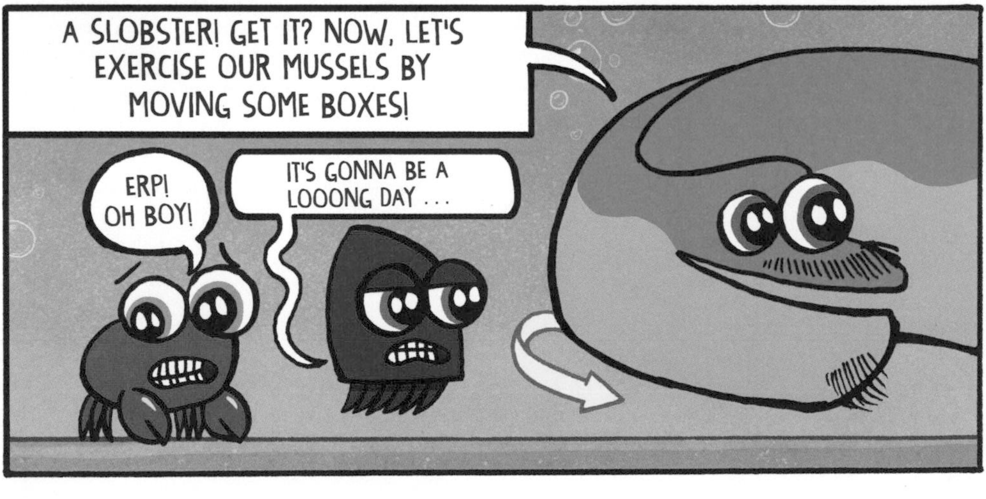
A SLOBSTER! GET IT? NOW, LET'S EXERCISE OUR MUSSELS BY MOVING SOME BOXES!
ERP! OH BOY!
IT'S GONNA BE A LOOONG DAY . . .

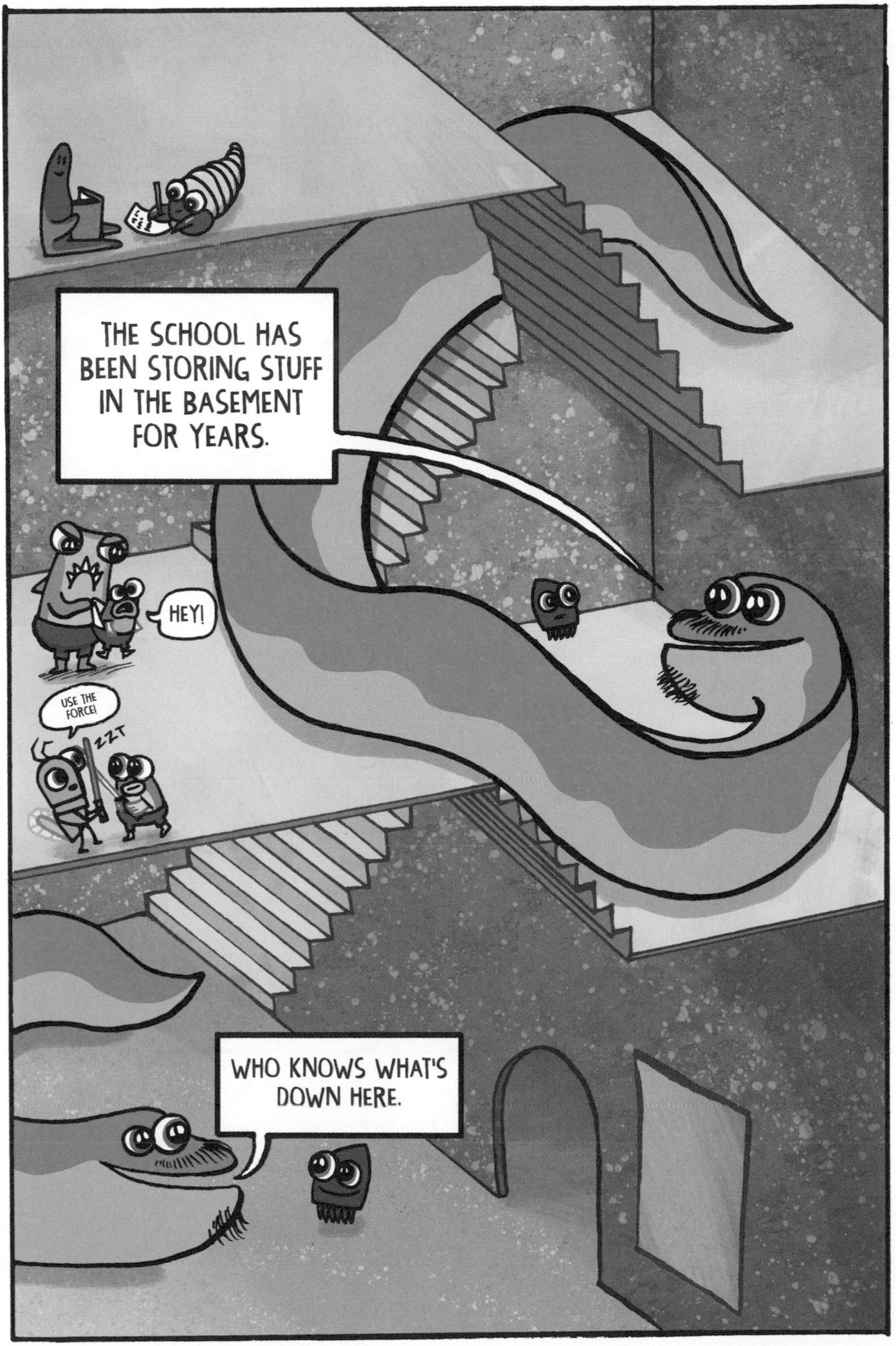
THE SCHOOL HAS BEEN STORING STUFF IN THE BASEMENT FOR YEARS.
HEY!
USE THE FORCE!
ZZT
WHO KNOWS WHAT'S DOWN HERE.

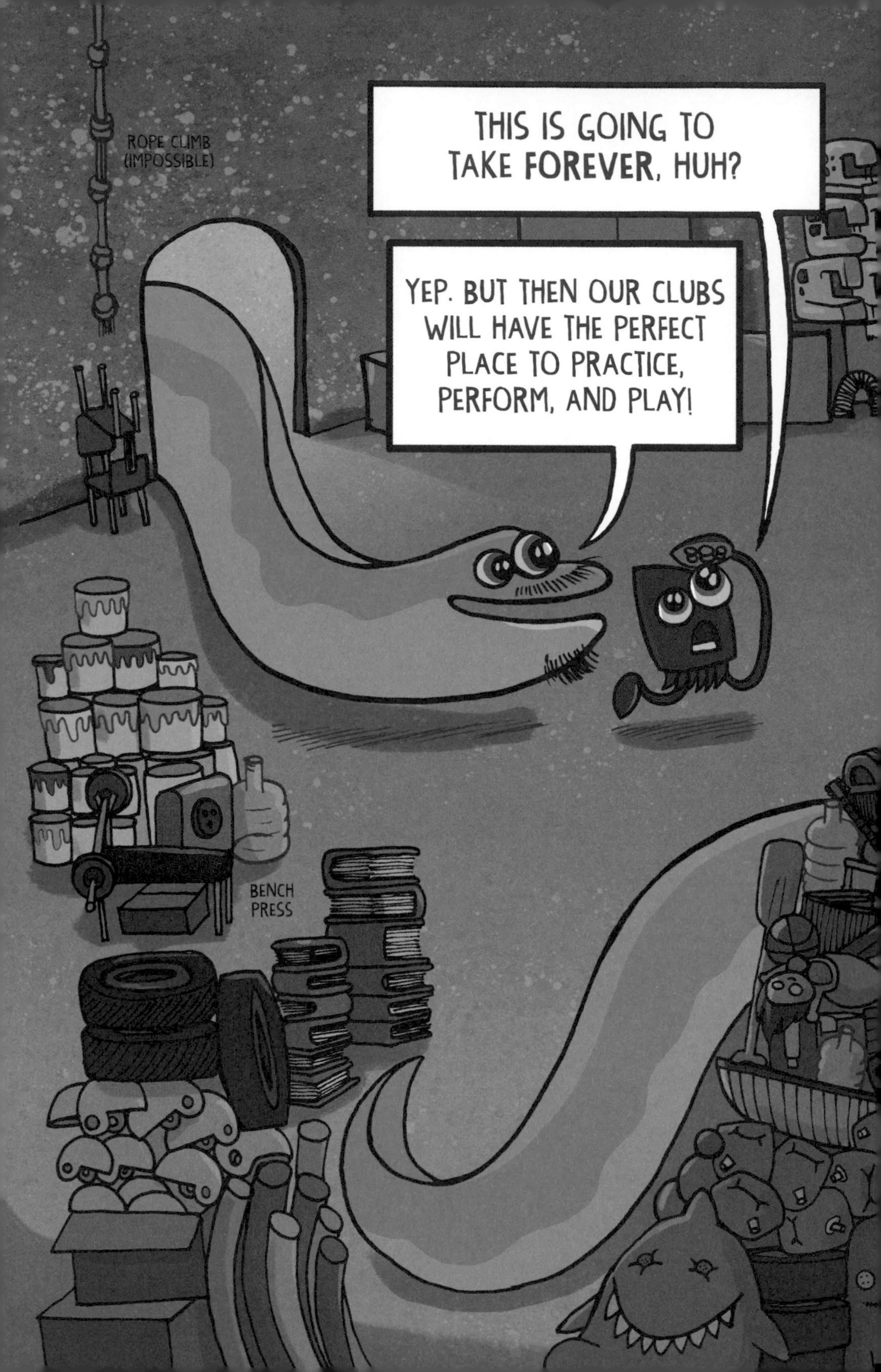
ROPE CLIMB (IMPOSSIBLE)
THIS IS GOING TO TAKE **FOREVER**, HUH?
YEP. BUT THEN OUR CLUBS WILL HAVE THE PERFECT PLACE TO PRACTICE, PERFORM, AND PLAY!
BENCH PRESS

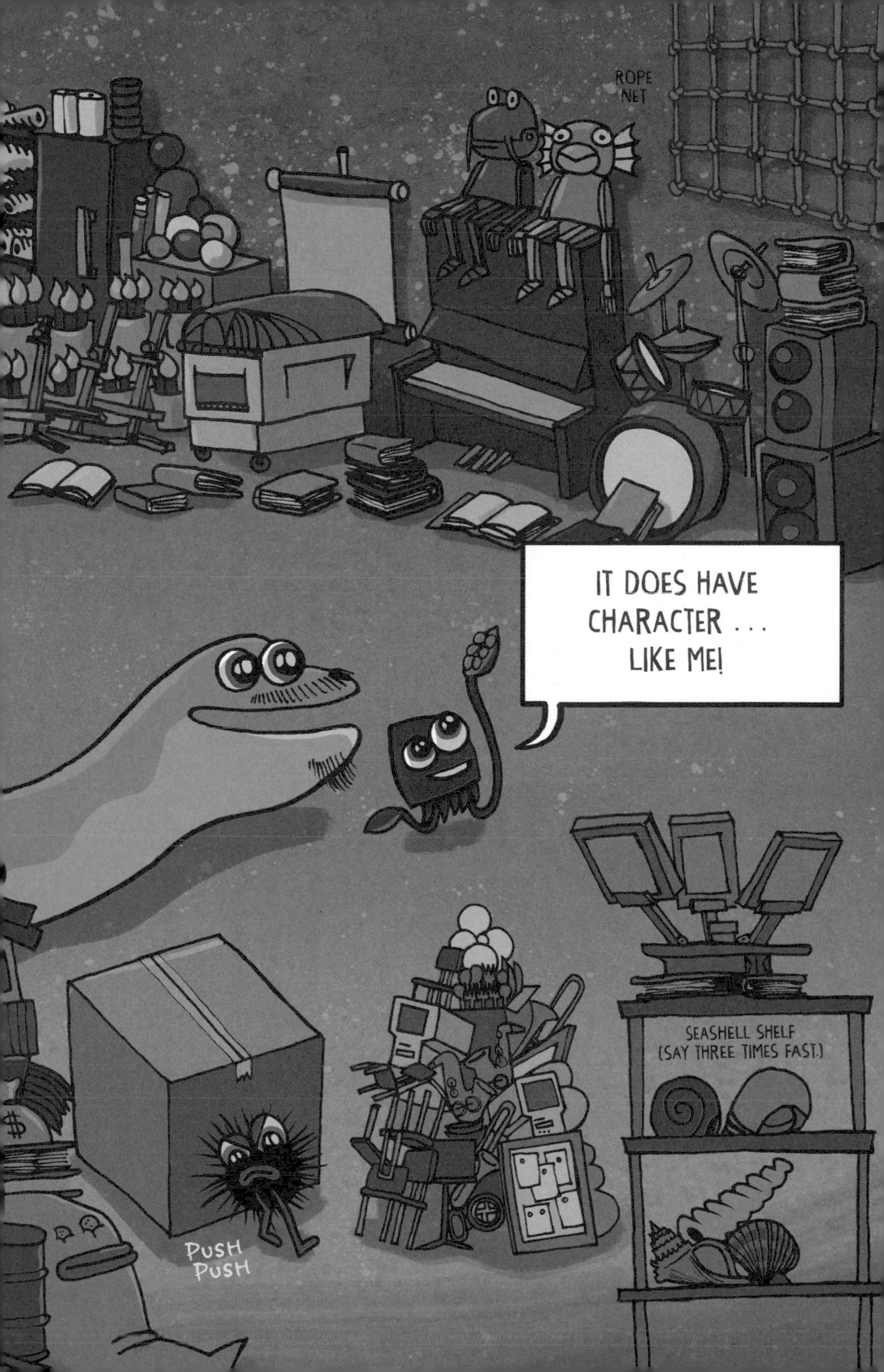
ROPE NET
IT DOES HAVE CHARACTER . . . LIKE ME!
SEASHELL SHELF (SAY THREE TIMES FAST.)
PUSH PUSH

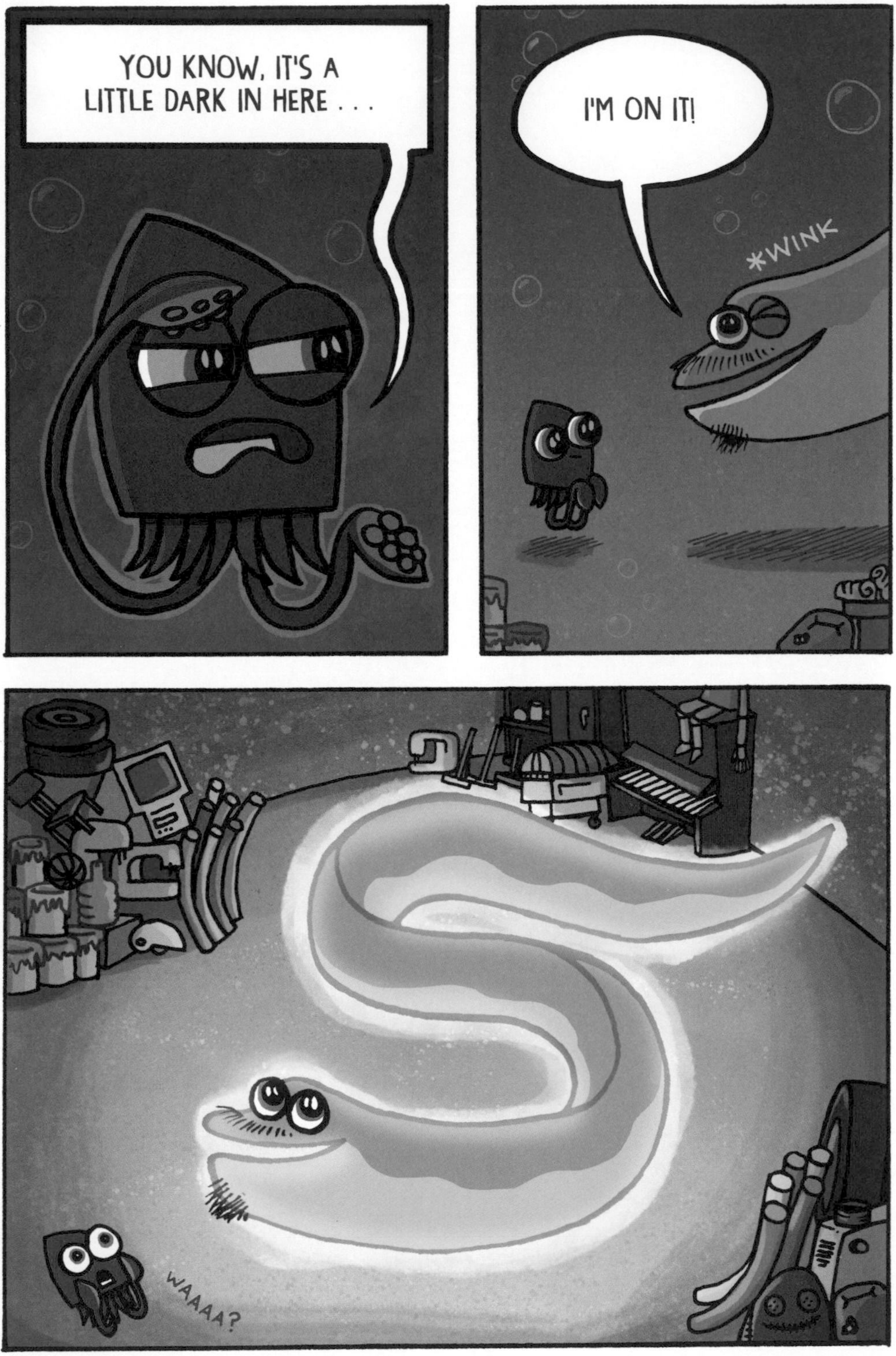

YOU KNOW, IT'S A LITTLE DARK IN HERE . . .
I'M ON IT!
*WINK
WAAAA?

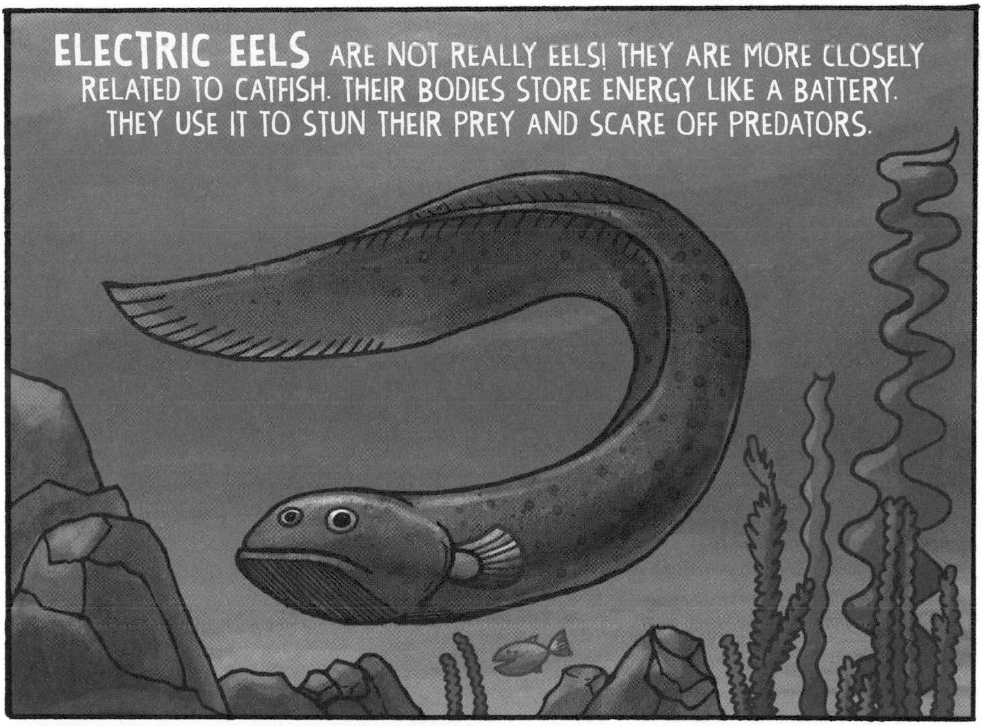
ELECTRIC EELS ARE NOT REALLY EELS! THEY ARE MORE CLOSELY RELATED TO CATFISH. THEIR BODIES STORE ENERGY LIKE A BATTERY. THEY USE IT TO STUN THEIR PREY AND SCARE OFF PREDATORS.

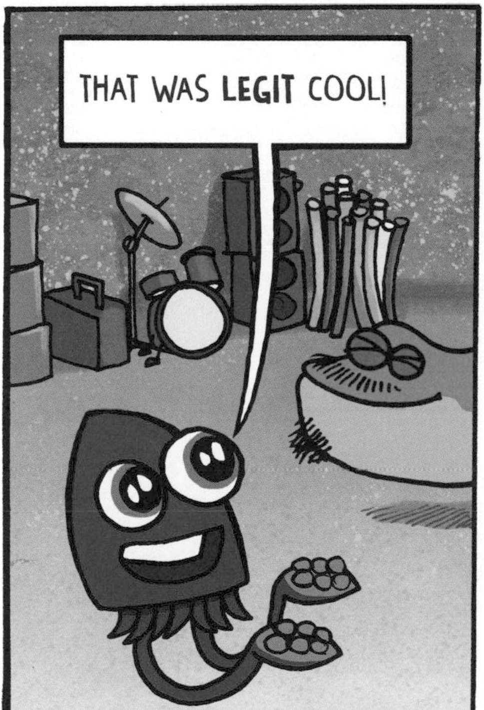
THAT WAS LEGIT COOL!

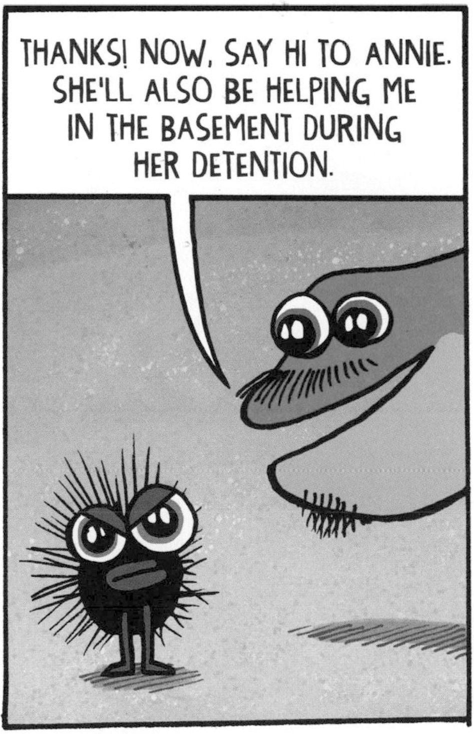
THANKS! NOW, SAY HI TO ANNIE. SHE'LL ALSO BE HELPING ME IN THE BASEMENT DURING HER DETENTION.

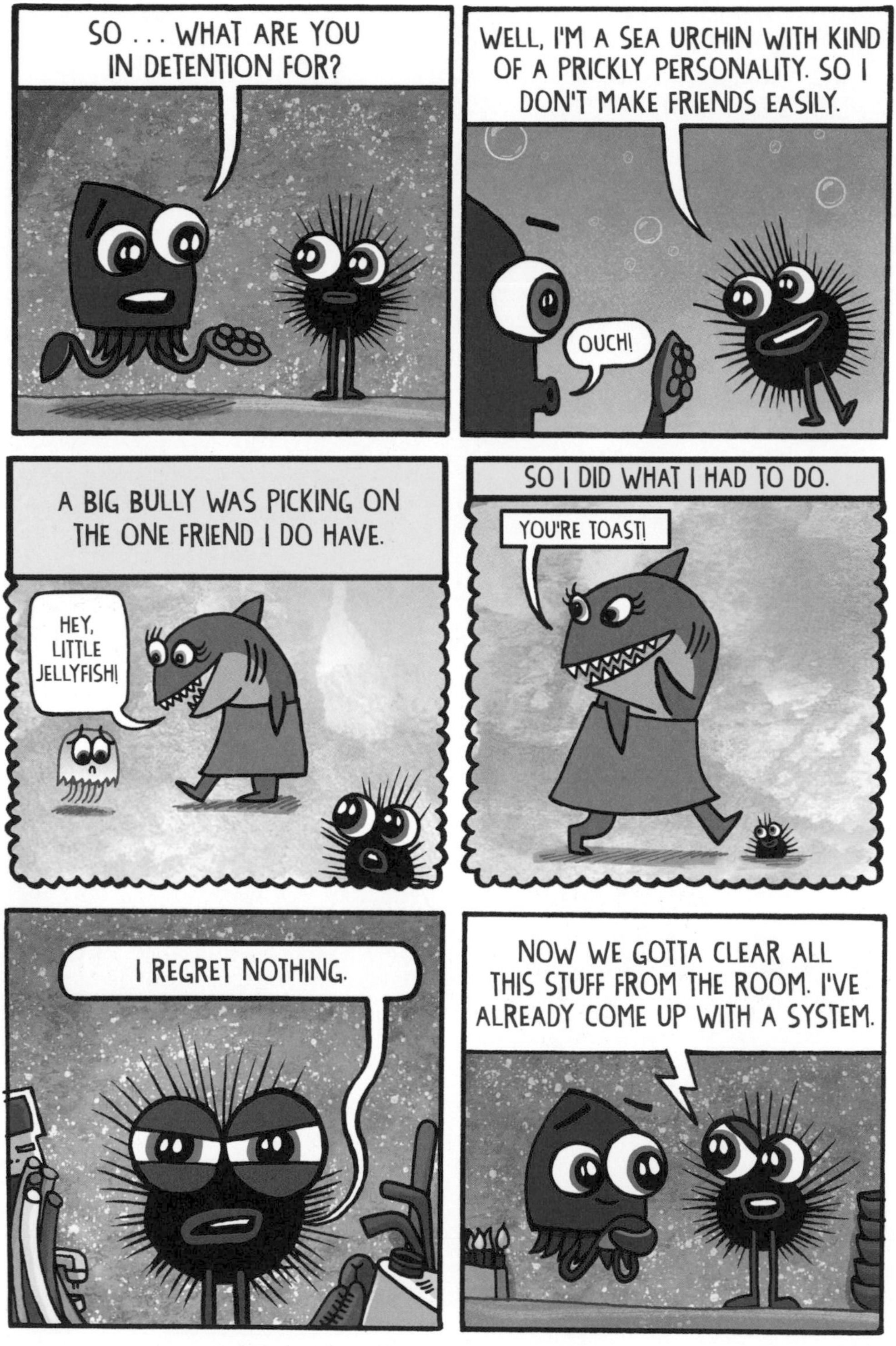
SO . . . WHAT ARE YOU IN DETENTION FOR?
WELL, I'M A SEA URCHIN WITH KIND OF A PRICKLY PERSONALITY. SO I DON'T MAKE FRIENDS EASILY.
OUCH!
A BIG BULLY WAS PICKING ON THE ONE FRIEND I DO HAVE.
HEY, LITTLE JELLYFISH!
SO I DID WHAT I HAD TO DO.
YOU'RE TOAST!
I REGRET NOTHING.
NOW WE GOTTA CLEAR ALL THIS STUFF FROM THE ROOM. I'VE ALREADY COME UP WITH A SYSTEM.

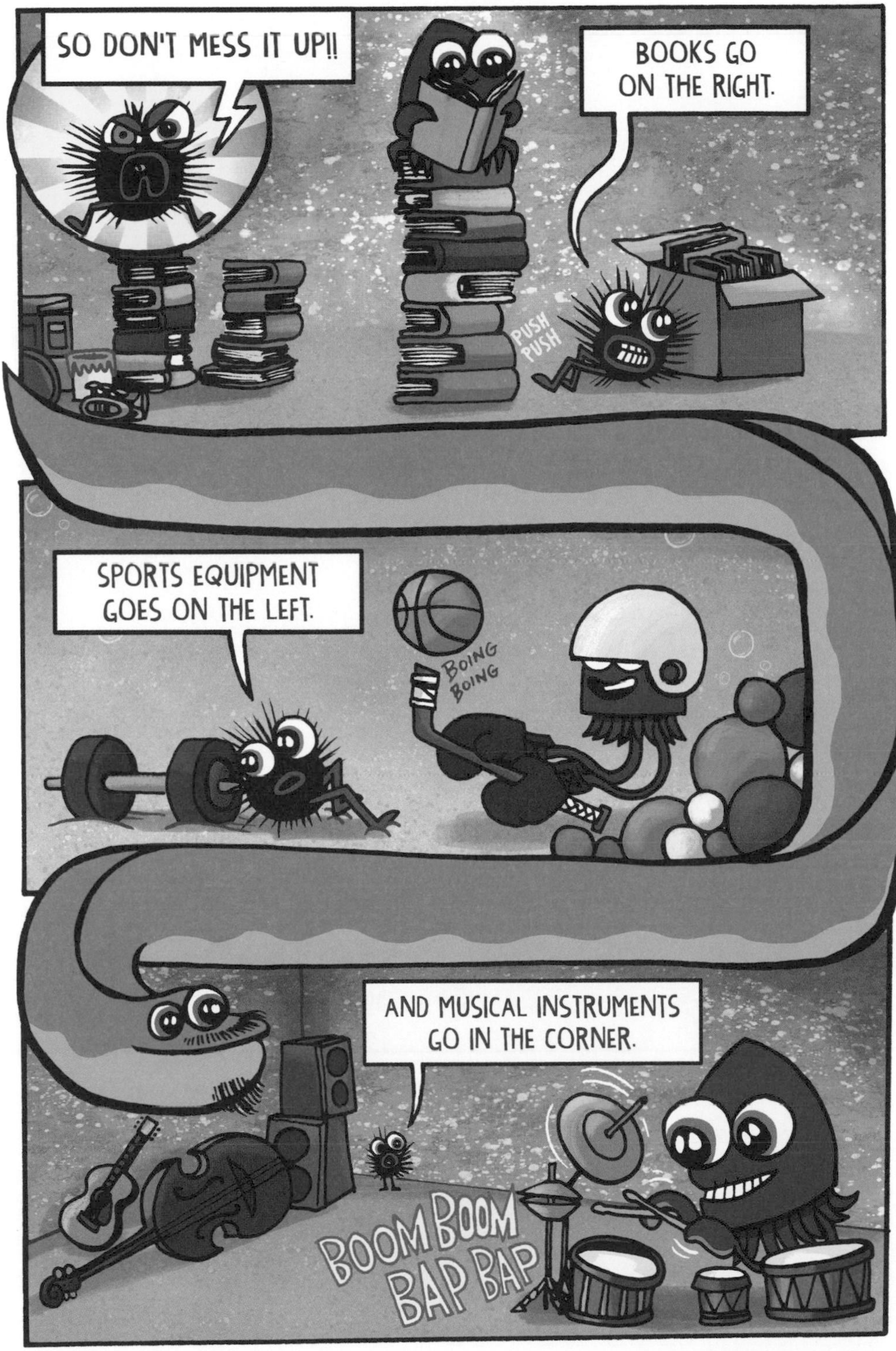
SO DON'T MESS IT UP!!
BOOKS GO ON THE RIGHT.
PUSH PUSH
SPORTS EQUIPMENT GOES ON THE LEFT.
BOING BOING
AND MUSICAL INSTRUMENTS GO IN THE CORNER.
BOOM BOOM BAP BAP

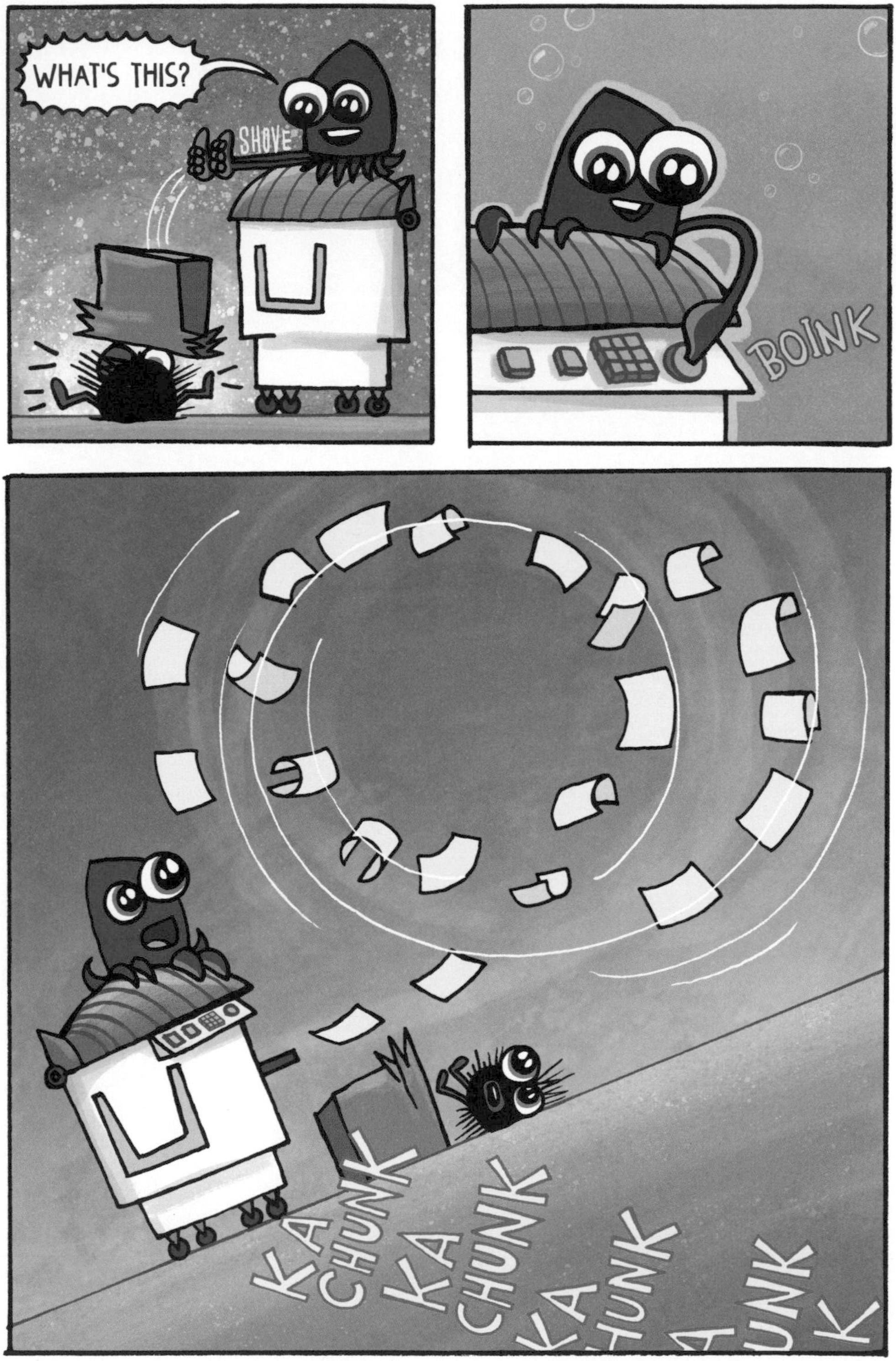
WHAT'S THIS?
SHOVE
BOINK
KA
CHUNK
KA
CHUNK
KA
CHUNK
KA
CHUNK
KA
CHUNK

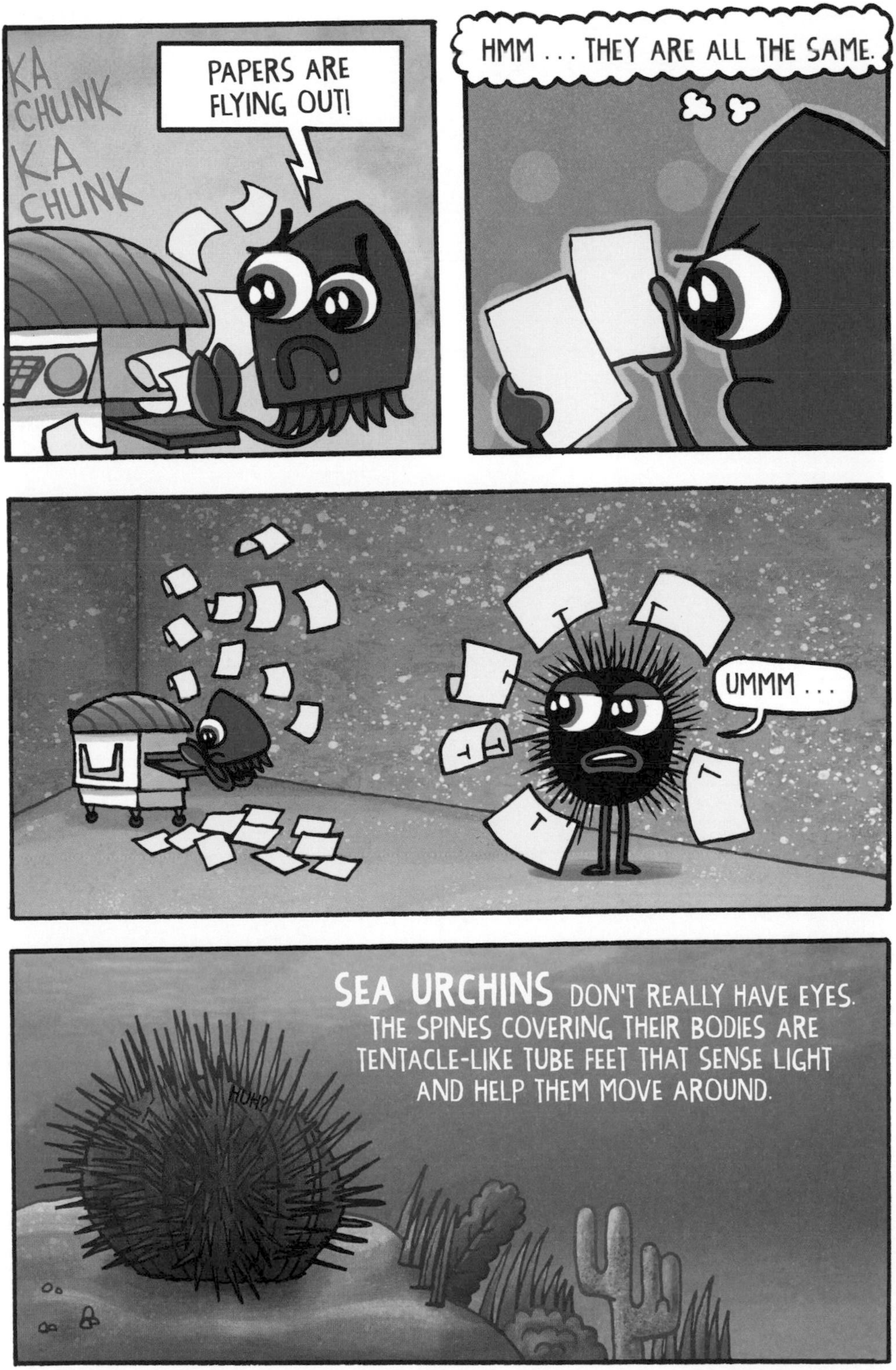
KA
CHUNK
KA
CHUNK
PAPERS ARE FLYING OUT!
HMM . . . THEY ARE ALL THE SAME.
UMMM . . .
SEA URCHINS DON'T REALLY HAVE EYES. THE SPINES COVERING THEIR BODIES ARE TENTACLE-LIKE TUBE FEET THAT SENSE LIGHT AND HELP THEM MOVE AROUND.
HUH?

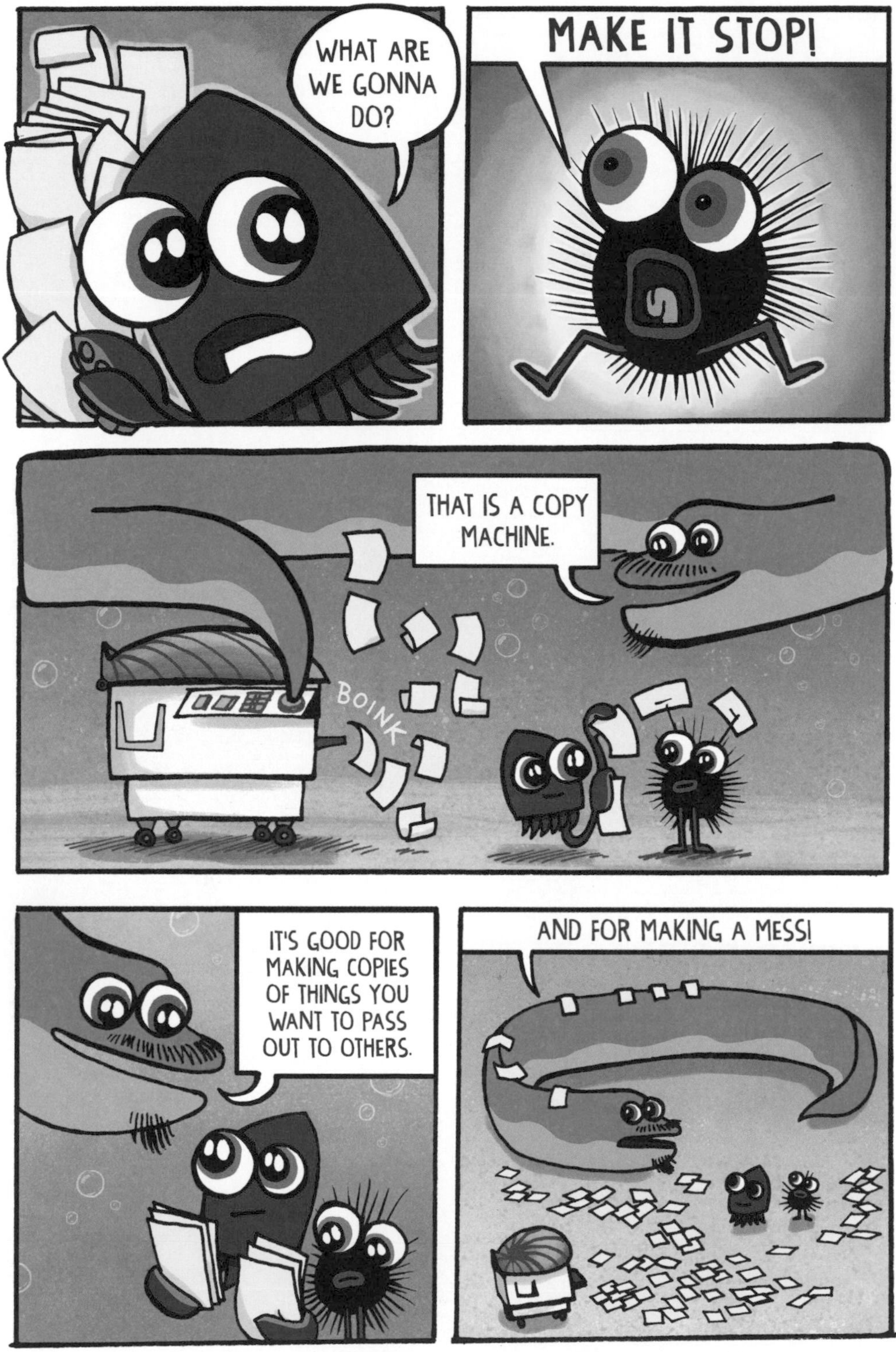
WHAT ARE WE GONNA DO?
MAKE IT STOP!
THAT IS A COPY MACHINE.
BOINK
IT'S GOOD FOR MAKING COPIES OF THINGS YOU WANT TO PASS OUT TO OTHERS.
AND FOR MAKING A MESS!

CHAPTER 4

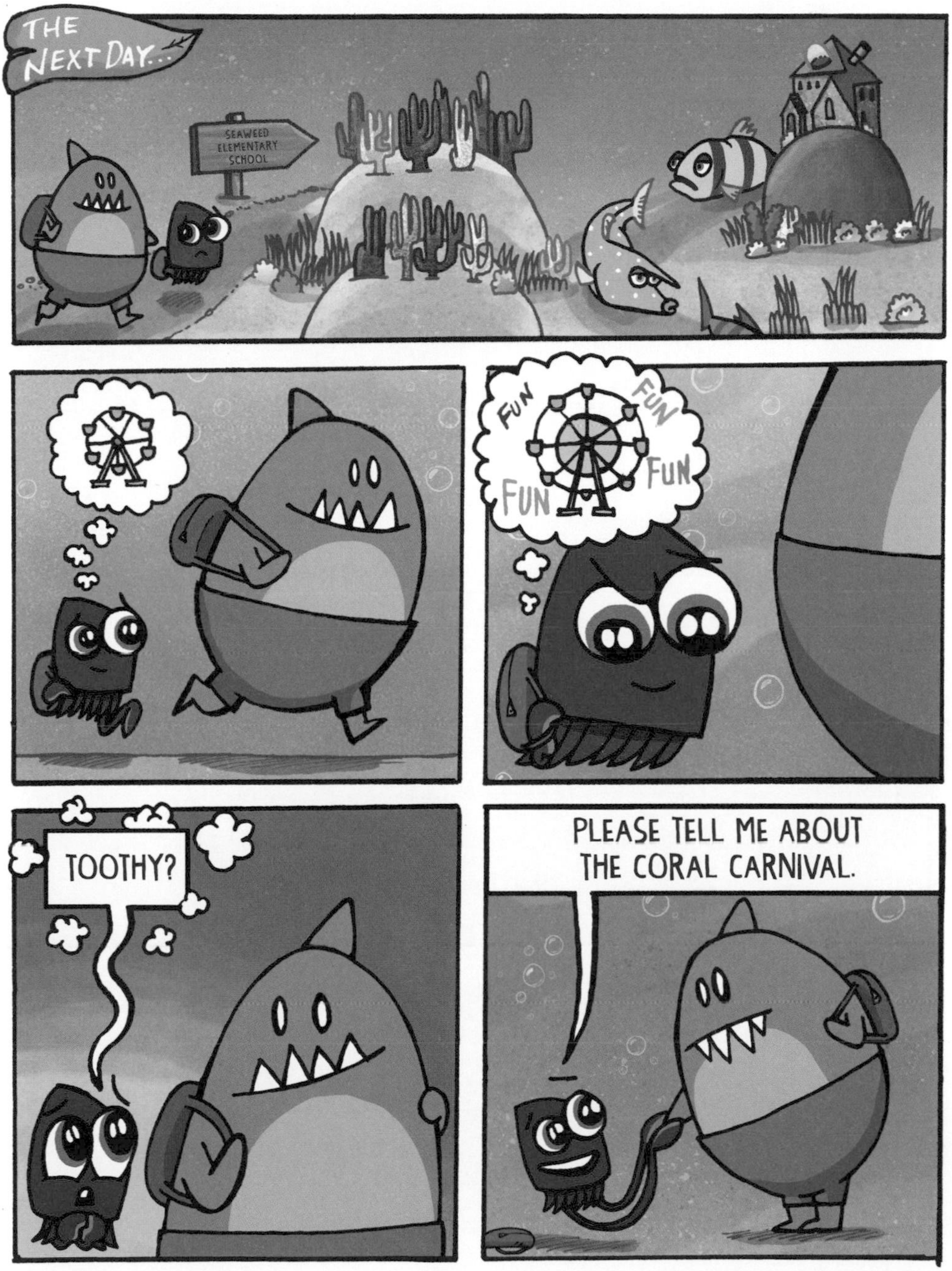
THE NEXT DAY...
SEAWEED ELEMENTARY SCHOOL
FUN
FUN
FUN
FUN
TOOTHY?
PLEASE TELL ME ABOUT THE CORAL CARNIVAL.

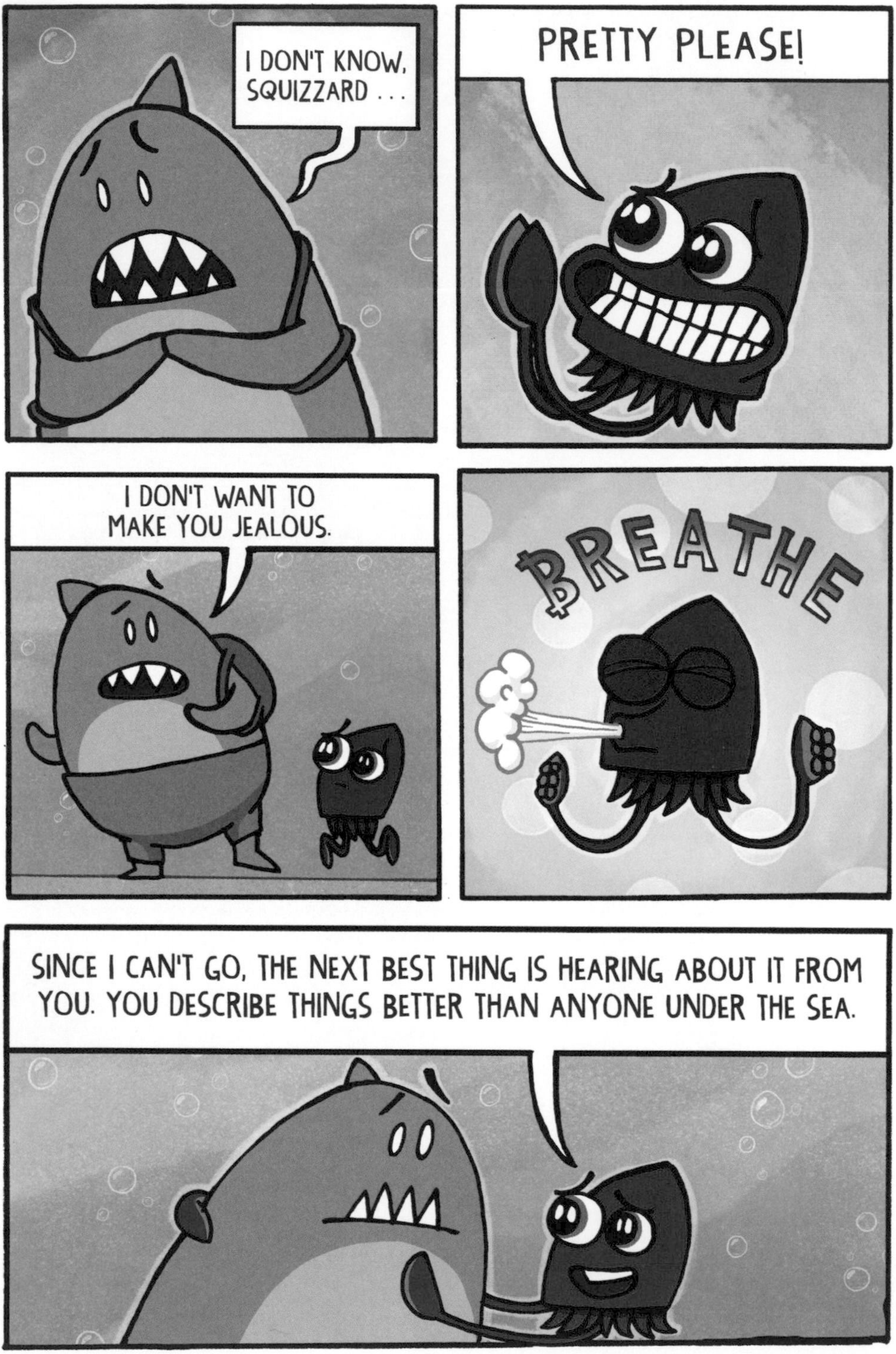
I DON'T KNOW, SQUIZZARD . . .
PRETTY PLEASE!
I DON'T WANT TO MAKE YOU JEALOUS.
BREATHE
SINCE I CAN'T GO, THE NEXT BEST THING IS HEARING ABOUT IT FROM YOU. YOU DESCRIBE THINGS BETTER THAN ANYONE UNDER THE SEA.

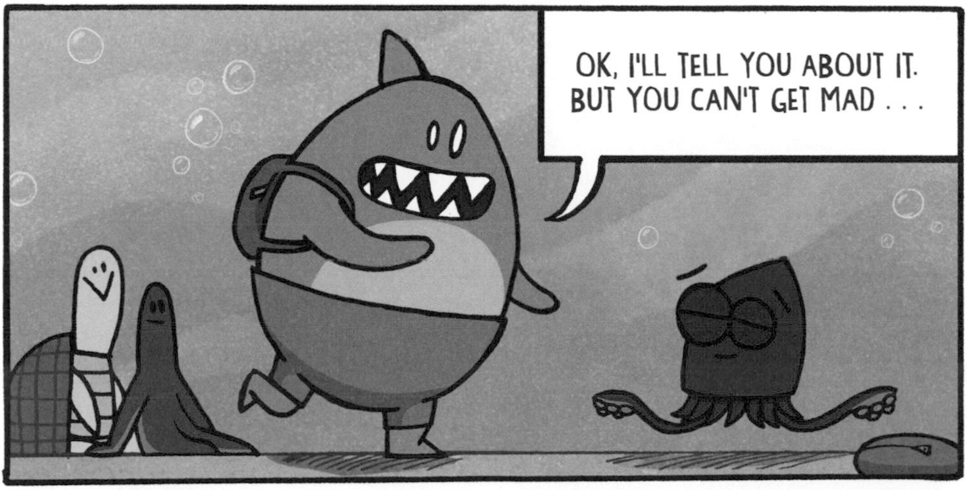
OK, I'LL TELL YOU ABOUT IT. BUT YOU CAN'T GET MAD . . .

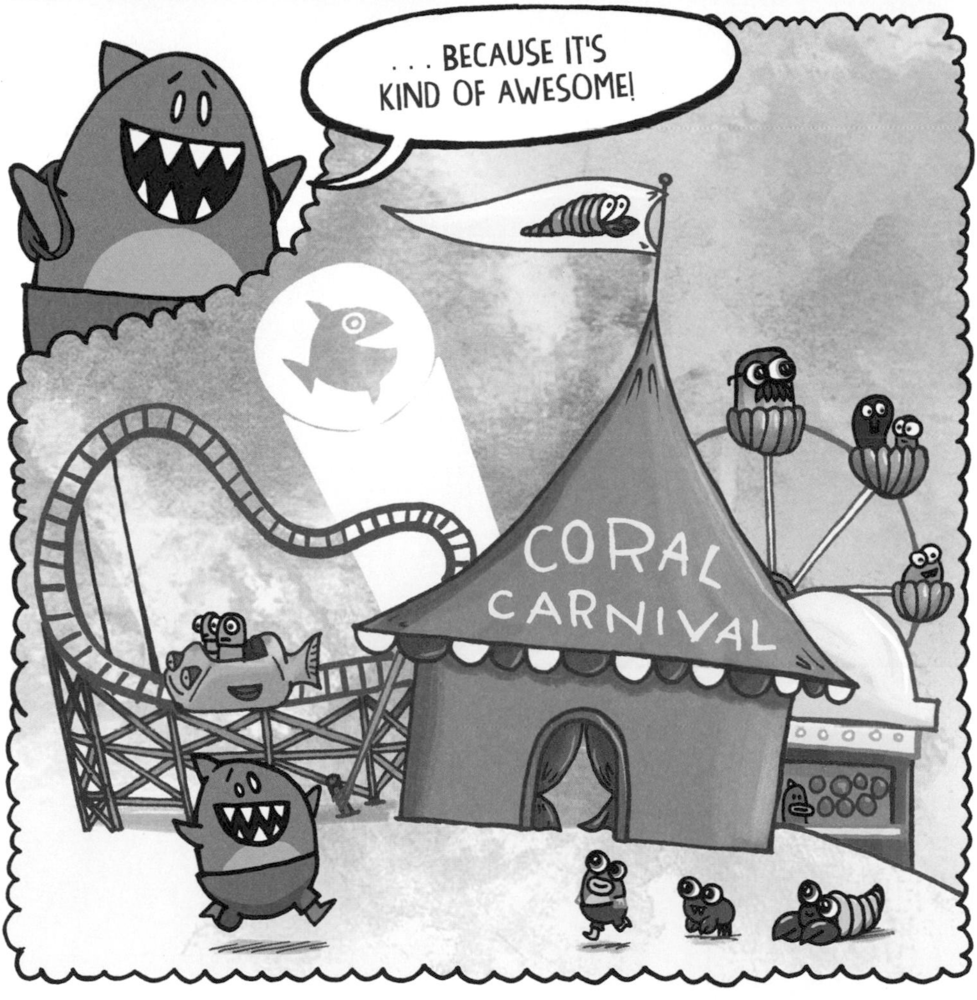
. . . BECAUSE IT'S KIND OF AWESOME!
CORAL CARNIVAL

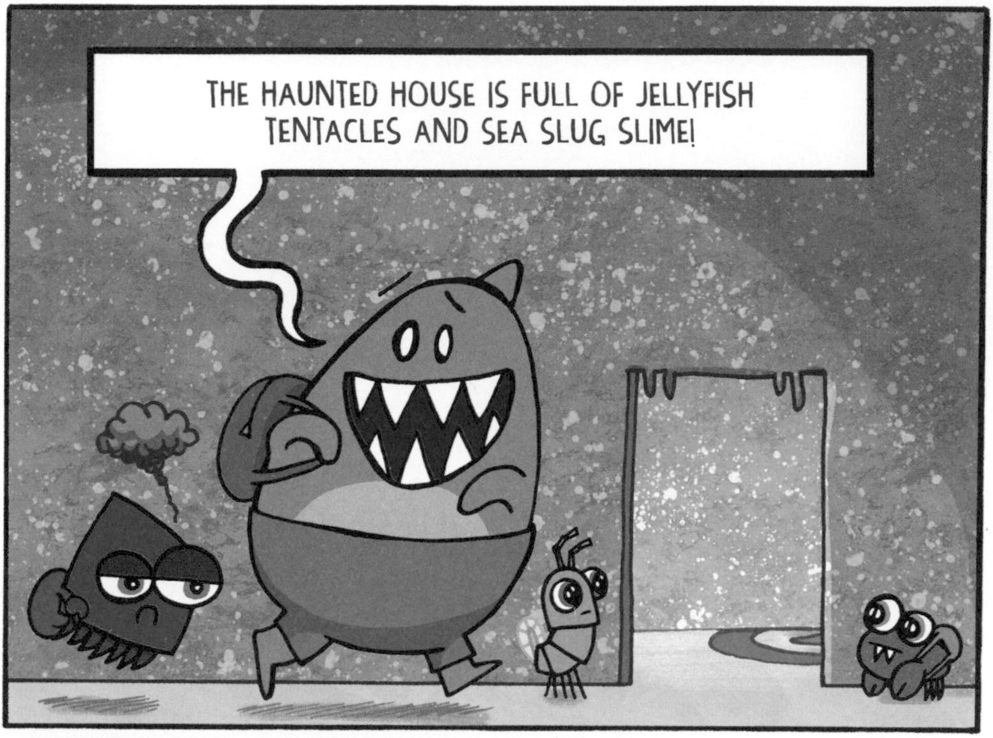
THE HAUNTED HOUSE IS FULL OF JELLYFISH TENTACLES AND SEA SLUG SLIME!

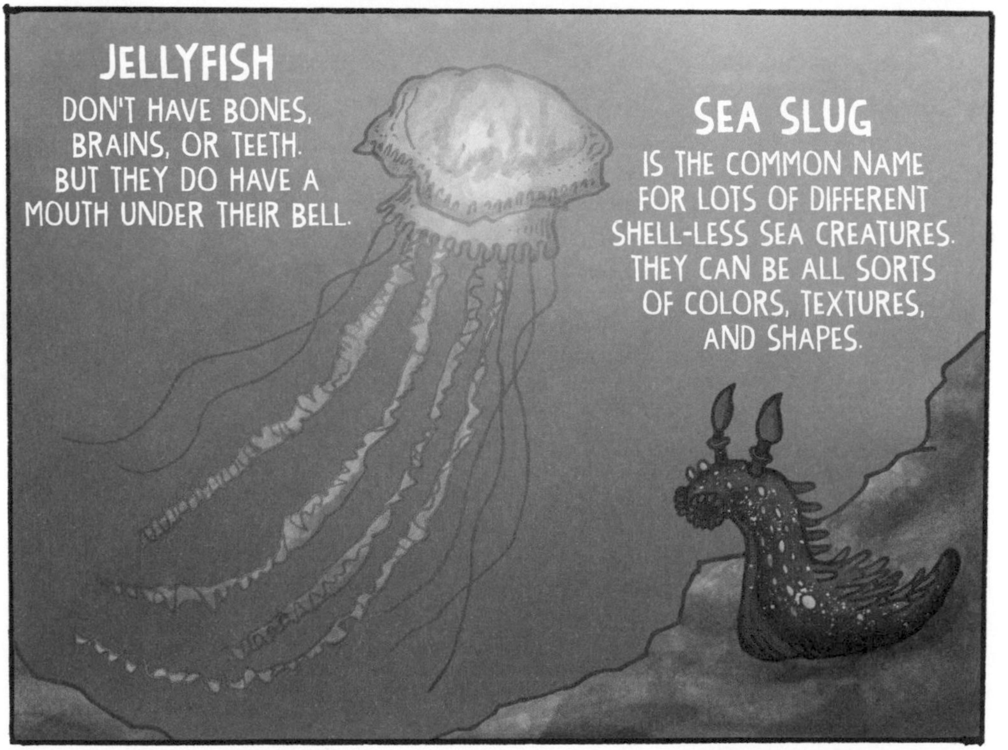
JELLYFISH
DON'T HAVE BONES, BRAINS, OR TEETH. BUT THEY DO HAVE A MOUTH UNDER THEIR BELL.
SEA SLUG
IS THE COMMON NAME FOR LOTS OF DIFFERENT SHELL-LESS SEA CREATURES. THEY CAN BE ALL SORTS OF COLORS, TEXTURES, AND SHAPES.

53

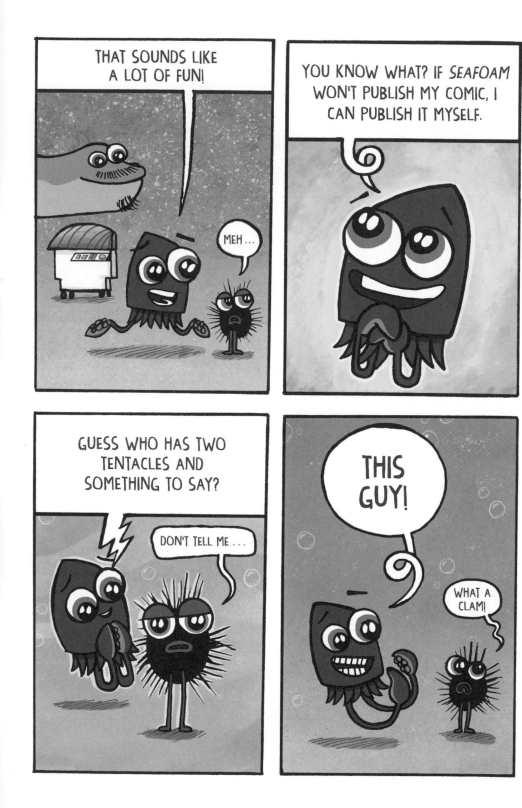

CHAPTER 5

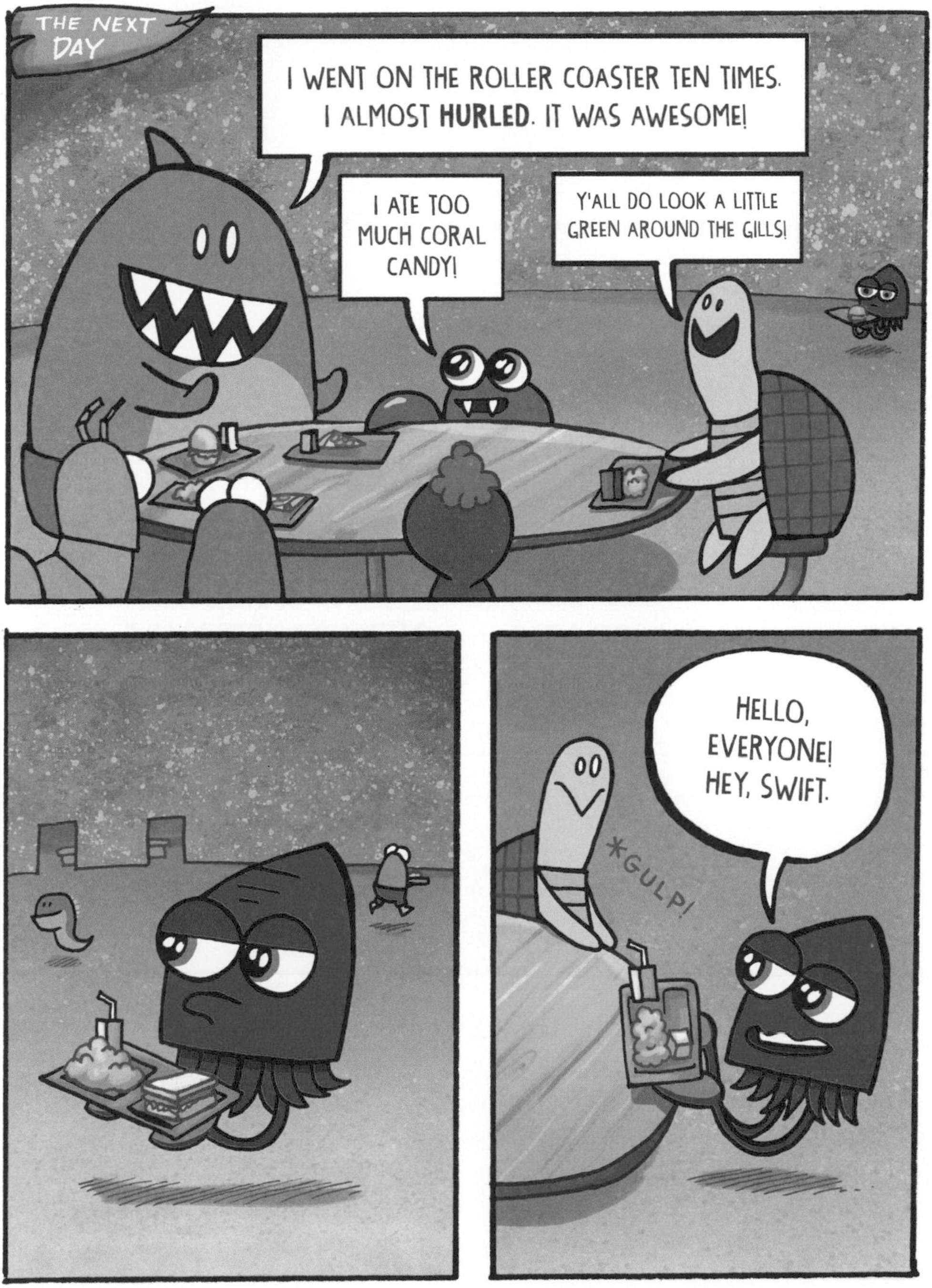
THE NEXT DAY
I WENT ON THE ROLLER COASTER TEN TIMES. I ALMOST **HURLED**. IT WAS AWESOME!
I ATE TOO MUCH CORAL CANDY!
Y'ALL DO LOOK A LITTLE GREEN AROUND THE GILLS!
*GULP!
HELLO, EVERYONE! HEY, SWIFT.

64

69

CHAPTER 6

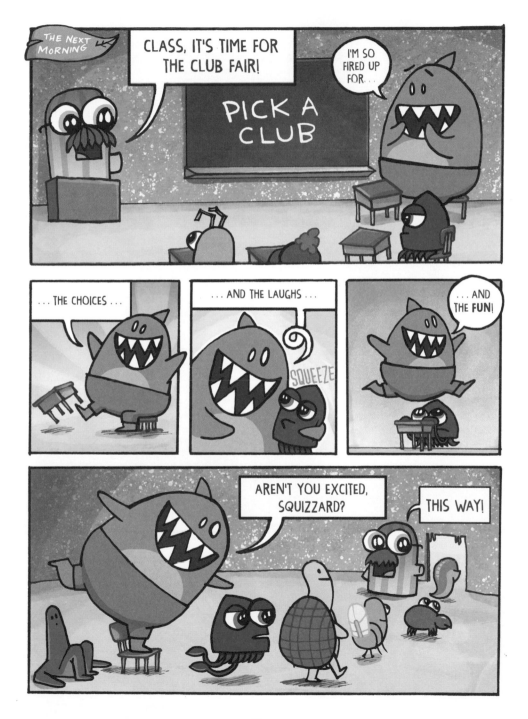

THE REAL SCOOP
BY TOOTHY

IT'S BEEN A BUSY WEEK IN THE DEEP REEF! THE TALENT SHOW IS IN JUST FIVE DAYS. I CAUGHT A PREVIEW OF NINA SEAL'S "SOMEWHERE UNDER A JET STREAM," AND IT DOESN'T DISAPPOINT!

GENERAL COMPLAINTS
BY ANNIE

WHEN WILL BRINEY BITES RETURN TO THE CAFETERIA VENDING MACHINE? THEY'VE BEEN OUT OF STOCK FOR OVER TWO WEEKS. THAT'S LONGER THAN TOOTHY'S ORAL REPORTS!

DEAR SHAY: ADVICE COLUMN

MY FRIEND IS MOVING AWAY AND I'M SAD. PLEASE HELP!
—KRISS

IT'S OK TO FEEL SAD. BUT JUST THINK: NOW YOU HAVE THE PERFECT PEN PAL AND A NEW PLACE TO VISIT!

TEN-TICKLES: A COMIC BY SQUIZZARD

GUPPY GOALS
BY DOUG

FIRST GRADE IS A WHIRLWIND! WRITING COMPLETE SENTENCES? KIND OF HARD. READING OUT LOUD? NERVE-RACKING! AND TELLING TIME? WHAT AM I, A SCIENTIST? BUT SCHOOL MEANS FRIENDS, SO I LOVE IT.

FIZZ'S TABLE

BREAKFAST IS IMPORTANT! SO I RECOMMEND THE CAFETERIA'S MORNING SMOOTHIE. MADE FROM BANANAS, APPLES, KELP, AND A DASH OF LOVE, THIS SWEET JUICE IS UNBE-REEF-ABLY GOOD!

INTERVIEW WITH PRINCIPAL OLGA KRAKEN BY TOOTHY

TOOTHY: WHY START AN AFTER-SCHOOL PROGRAM? P. OK: SO MANY OF OUR STUDENTS ARE TALENTED. CLUBS ARE GREAT PLACES TO SHARE THOSE GIFTS.

PHOTOS
BY SWIFT

FACULTY ADVISER:
JALEEL ALI

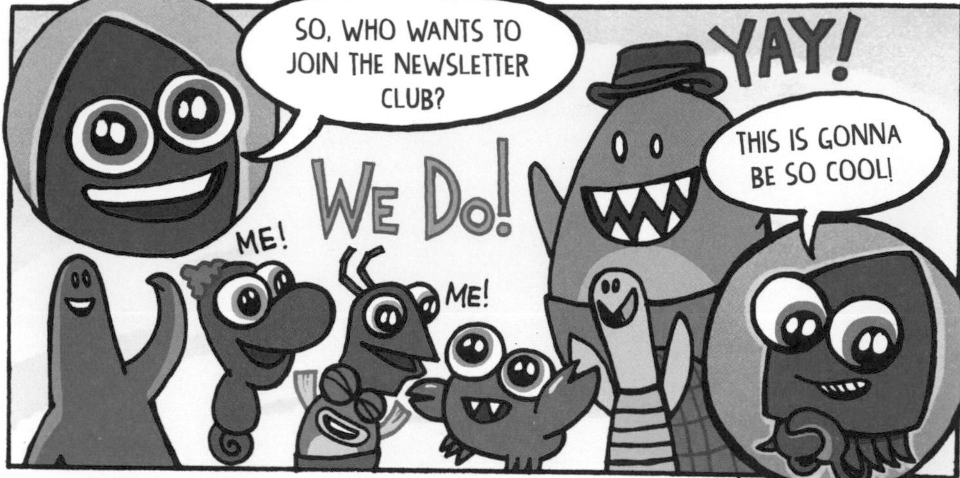
SO, WHO WANTS TO JOIN THE NEWSLETTER CLUB?
WE DO!
ME!
ME!
YAY!
THIS IS GONNA BE SO COOL!

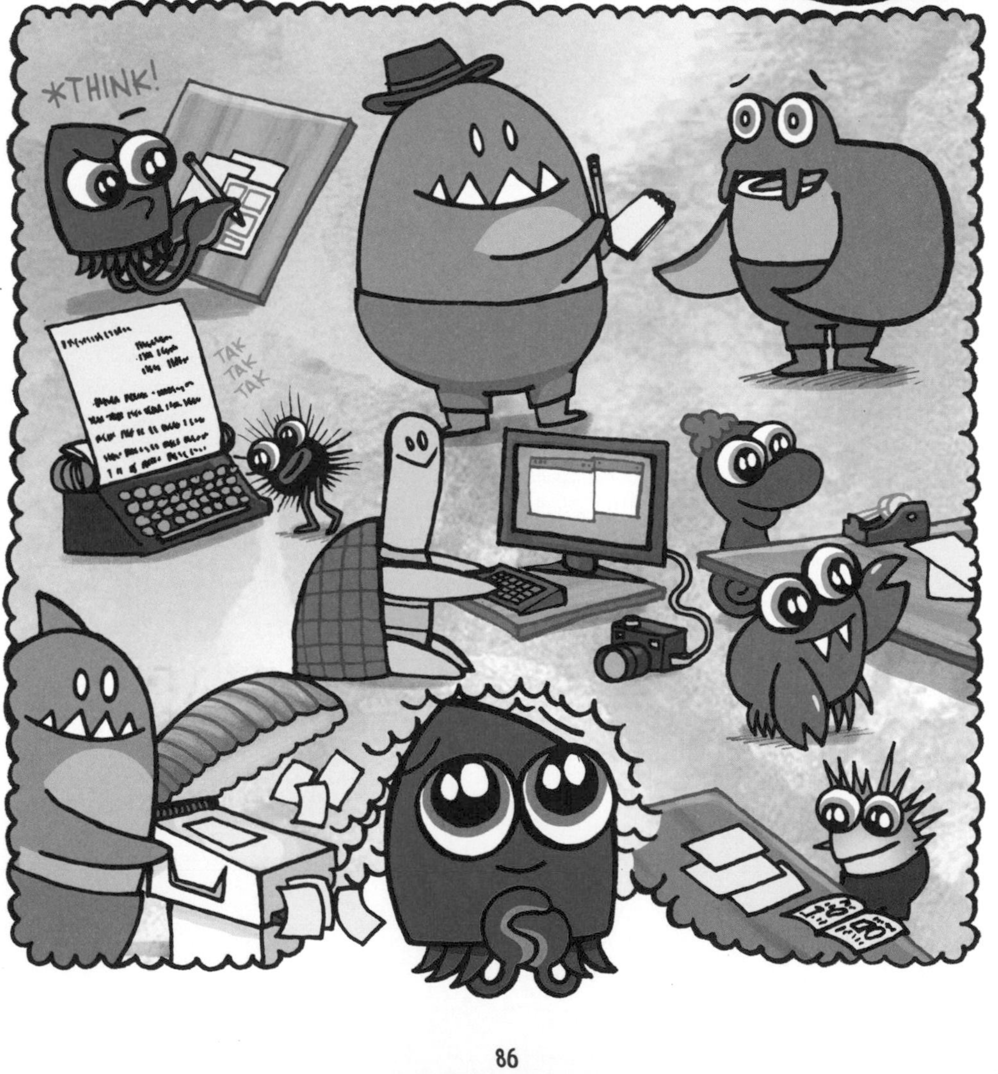
*THINK!
TAK TAK TAK

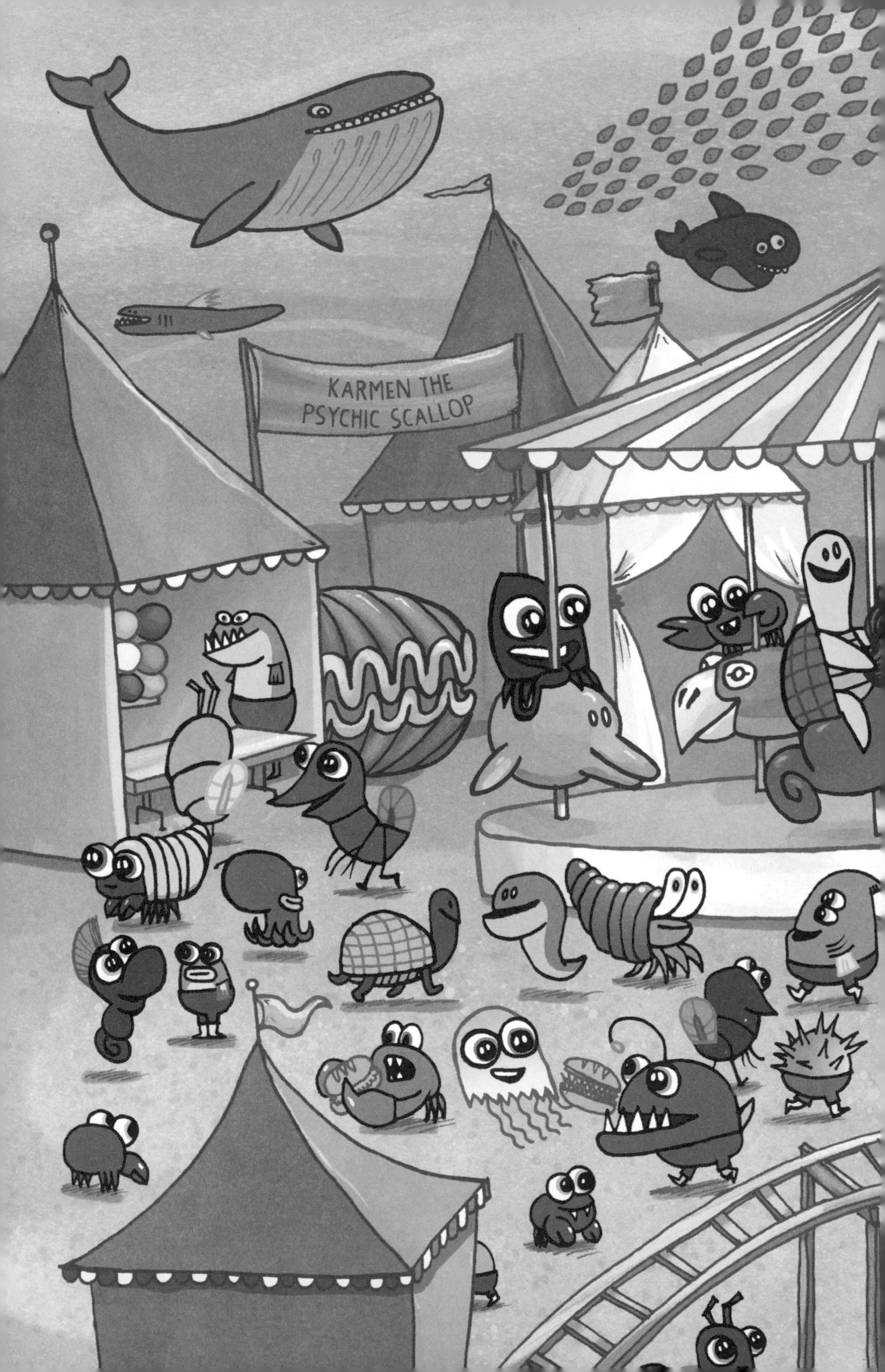
KARMEN THE
PSYCHIC SCALLOP

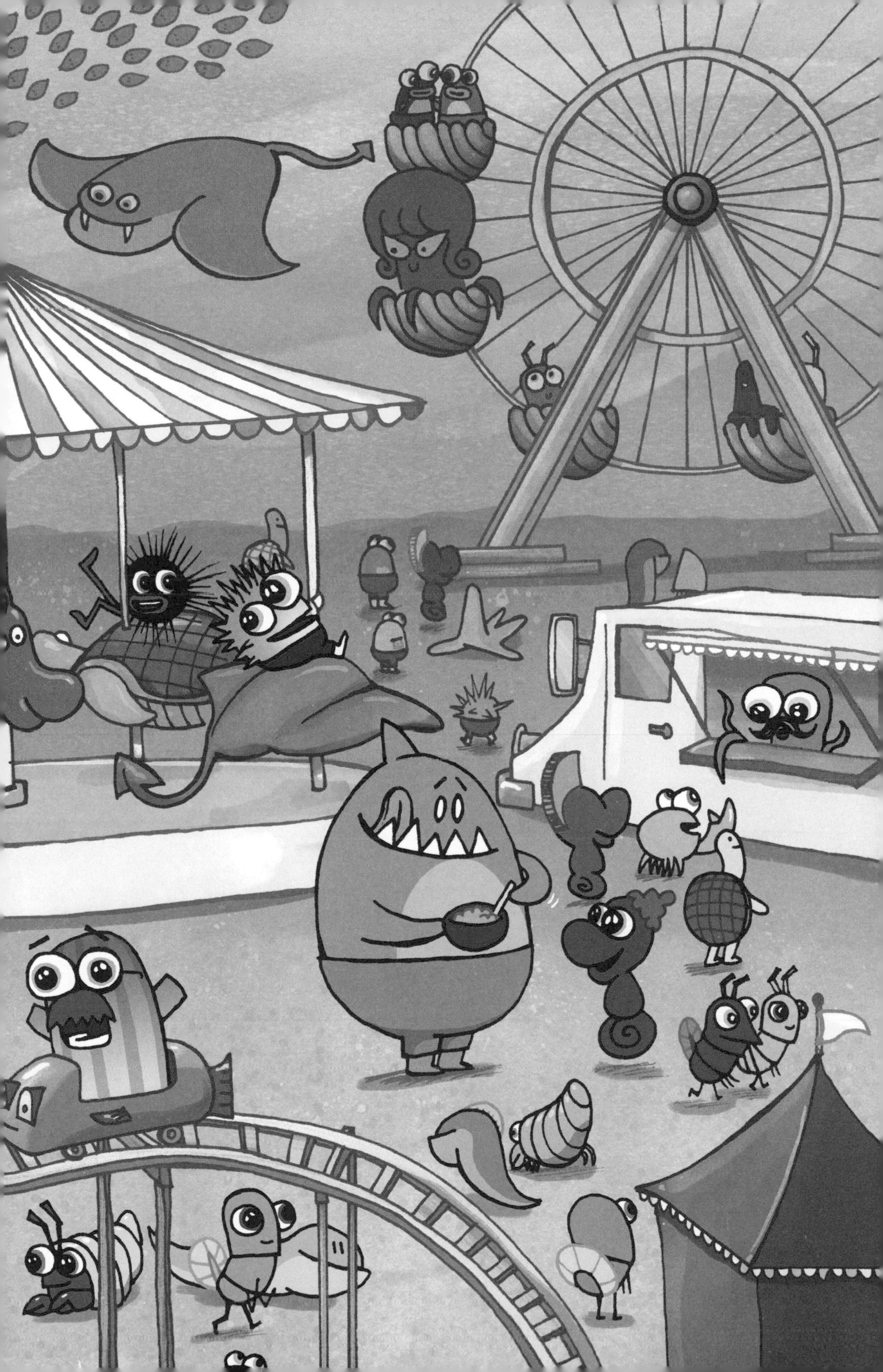

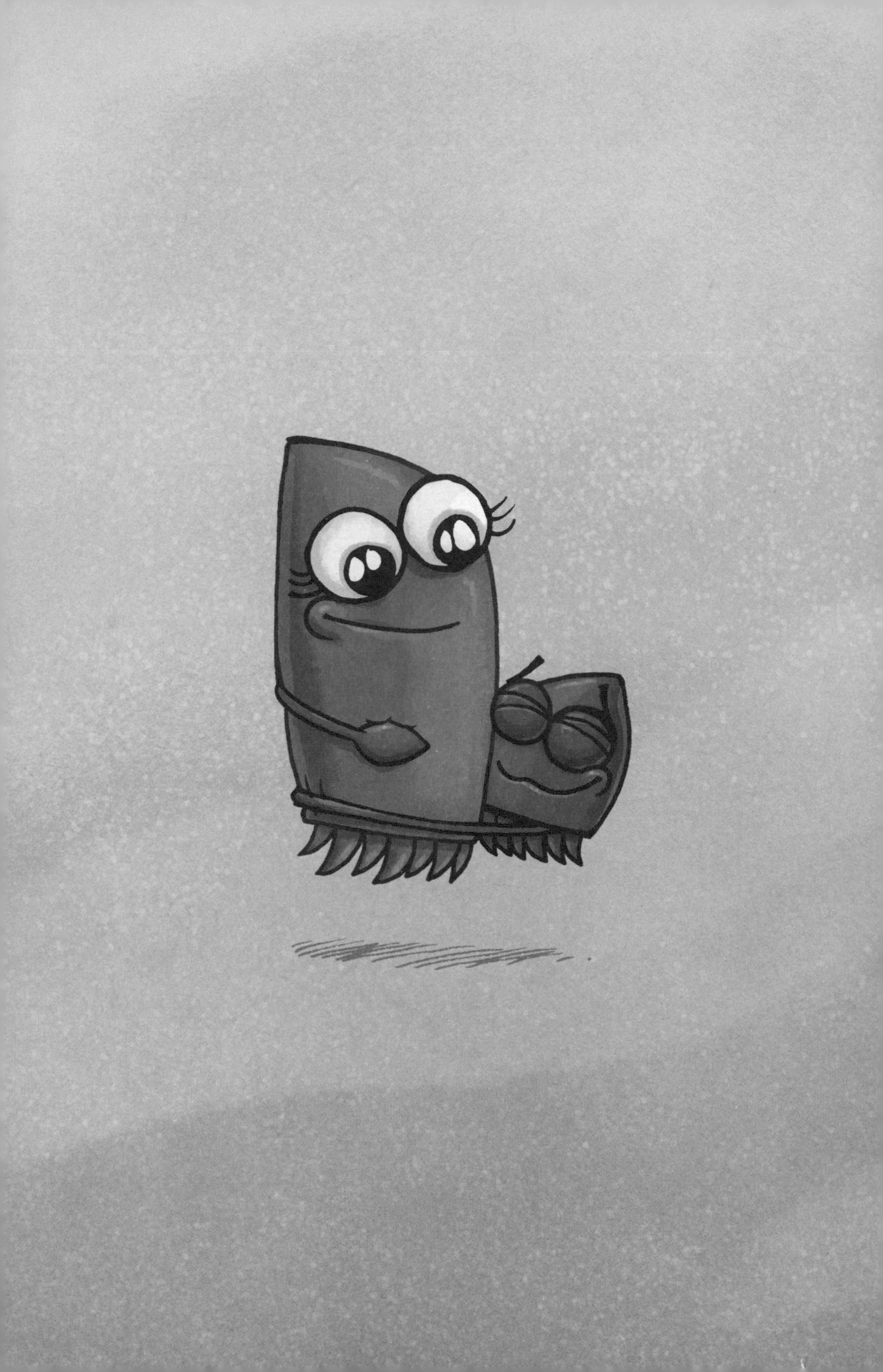

A CARNIVAL OF CORAL

Coral reefs are important underwater communities. They are structures made from the skeletons of tiny sea creatures called coral. Coral reefs cover less than 2% of the ocean floor, but around 25% of all ocean life depends on them for food and shelter. Pollution, rising water temperatures, and other factors are destroying coral reefs. Some scientists want to help by building artificial (ar-tih-FISH-ul), or man-made, reefs.

Artificial reefs can be made from all kinds of materials, like shipwrecks, sunken planes and lighthouses, concrete blocks, or even old tires. They give coral and sea plants a place to grow and fish a place to live and lay their eggs. If artificial reefs are not properly planned, they can pollute the ocean. It's a good thing Mr. Jaleel built his artificial reef carnival so carefully!

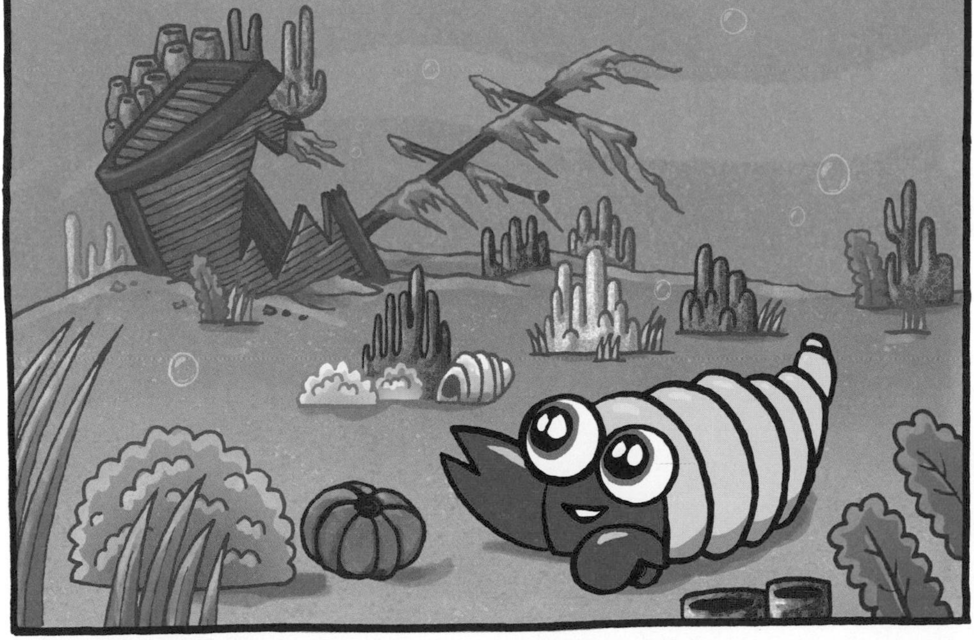

MAKE YOUR OWN NEWSLETTER!

You don't need to wait until you are an adult to publish your art and writing. You only need a pencil and paper! But ask a grown-up to help if you want to use other supplies: crayons, rubber stamps, stickers, tape, glue, and other art supplies.

CRAYONS

1 Decide what interests you.

2 Fold your paper into a book.

3 Write stories, essays, poems, or reviews.

4 Draw comics or paste in pictures and decorations.

5 Your newsletter is done!

KEVIN SHERRY is the author and illustrator of many children's picture books, most notably The Yeti Files and Remy Sneakers series, and the picture book I'M THE BIGGEST THING IN THE OCEAN, which received starred reviews and won an original artwork award from the Society of Illustrators. He's a man of many interests: a chef, an avid cyclist and screen printer, and a performer of hilarious puppet shows for kids and adults. Kevin lives in Baltimore, Maryland.

ACKNOWLEDGMENTS

Thanks To Rachel Orr, Cathy, James, Brian, Margie, Amelia, Dan, Al, Devlin, Gerrit, William, Sam, and Charlotte James. This book is inspired in part by the Zine Club at the Baltimore Design School, the Print and Multiples Fair that happens there, and Kevin's love of small press expos everywhere.

Ruby

Kinkos